Lesley Dimmlie

A Hangman's Delight...

An escaped killer changes his identity but not his
instincts. . . .

A daring crook has a handsome haul and no place
to spend it. . . .

A dying girl leaves a clue that foils an almost
perfect crime. . . .

A case of mistaken identity leads to a case of
mistaken murder. . . .

A victimized schoolboy turns the tables on his
tormentor. . . .

A sinister artist paints his best portraits in blood
red. . . .

Hard Day at the Scaffold

Alfred Hitchcock

A DELL BOOK

Published by
Dell Publishing Co., Inc.
1 Dag Hammarskjold Plaza
New York, New York 10017

Dell ® TM 681510, Dell Publishing Co., Inc.

ISBN: 0-440-13434-X

Printed in the United States of America
Two Previous Dell Editions
New Dell Edition
December 1985

ACKNOWLEDGMENTS

THE BABY by Jonathan Craig—Copyright © 1964 by H.S.D.
Publications, Inc. Reprinted by permission of the author and
the author's agents, Scott Meredith Literary Agency, Inc.
DON'T LIVE IN A COFFIN by Helen Nielsen—Copyright ©1960
by H.S.D. Publications, Inc. Reprinted by permission of the
author and the author's agents, Scott Meredith Literary
Agency, Inc.
A HUNDRED TIMES by Syd Hoff—Copyright ©1966 by H.S.D.
Publications, Inc. Reprinted by permission of the author and
the author's agents, Scott Meredith Literary Agency, Inc.

CONTENTS

INTRODUCTION

If you had happened to be in the vicinity of my garden one recent Sunday morning at about 2 A.M.—though I'm sure you weren't, since I was quite alone at the time—you would have noted that I was disturbed and even distraught. I frowned; my jaw was set; and, as I walked, I kicked out every now and then at innocent leaves and pebbles in my path.

I had, you see, been grossly insulted just a few hours before.

The incident took place at a small dinner party at my home, a party Mrs. Hitchcock and I had given for some friends and some friends of friends. The man who caused the incident was a friend of a friend, a person I had never met before; and I realize now, thinking back over it, that I really had not liked the look of him as he sat across the table from me ladling in my soup and making two of my best sirloin steaks disappear. But I am, I like to think, a charitable man and a good host, and so I did nothing more than smile pleasantly at the man—totally unprepared for what was coming—as he approached me after dinner and maneuvered me off into a corner.

And then it came. He put a jovial, bearlike arm around my shoulders, causing my knees to buckle, breathed the fumes of my fifty-year-old brandy into my face, and said, "You know what's wrong with your pictures and television shows, Hitchcock?"

It took me at least a full minute to answer, and I must admit that my voice was both icy and bleak. "I was unaware," I said, "that there's *anything* wrong with my films and television shows."

"Well, there is," the monster said, comfortably using his free hand to pat his stomach stuffed with *my* food. "And I'll tell you the trouble in just a couple of sentences. You're concerned only with crime and violence—everything in your stuff is shooting and stabbing and hanging and people falling down stairs. You ought to try to do things that are a little more cultural." And then he let me go and walked away, but not before he had delivered the *coup de grace*. "But people like you, I guess," he said, "are just not culturally inclined."

The reader, I know, will find the incident hard to believe, but I assure you that it actually happened. Can you imagine it—the absolute blindness of the man? *Me*—concerned only with crime and violence? *Me*—not culturally inclined? I didn't know whether to laugh or cry, thinking about it later as I walked around my garden, that someone could say these things about a man who had won no fewer than *two* gold medals, one for Flower Arrangement and the other for Neatest Notebook in the Music Appreciation Class, back at school.

Naturally, I had managed to shrug off the incident by the time I finally got to bed at about 5 A.M. But it *did* bother me for a while, and I'll tell you truthfully that the memory still returns to upset me every now and then. As a result, I've decided that I must, in some public way, make it clear that I am as cultural as anybody, and more so than many. This space seems to be the perfect opportunity—and so, if the reader will bear with me, I intend now to put aside the remarks originally intended for this introduction and devote the remainder of these pages to a discussion of my five favorite modern paintings—paintings which I urge all of you to see as you visit the world's most important museums. (And I'd like to see my friend with the brandy breath come up with something more cultural than *that!*)

The list of my all-time favorites follows:

1. *Sugar Cane* by Diego Rivera. (Now there's a really beautiful painting, with those Mexican workers in a colorful sugar field, curved knives flashing as several of them cut the cane. You know, I can see the start of a great movie. Let's say that one of those workers suddenly turns on another, his ominous knife lifted in the air . . .)

2. *The Battle of the Insects* by André Masson. (Let's see, now—if some radiation force would make those insects the size of New York skyscrapers . . .)

3. *Living Still Life* by Salvador Dali. (Notice the way

that knife in the painting seems to be rising—all by itself —from the table into the air? I wonder if anyone has ever done a film about a vengeful knife—a knife with a will and a blood-lust of its own?)

4. *Mardi Gras* by Paul Cézanne. (Nobody can match Cézanne's color sense, absolutely nobody. But why has Cézanne composed his painting that way, with the two figures walking in Red Indian, single-file style, and with the rear figure's hand half-hidden and curved as though he's clutching something? Could the thing he's holding be a gun?)

5. *Head of a Young Man* by Pablo Picasso. (Well, after all, Picasso named it—not me. Not a whole young man, take note; just a head. Just a head lying there, detached from the body but still alive—alive and thinking its evil, malevolent thoughts. . . .)

I trust that the foregoing will deal once and for all with the man who attacked me so heartlessly at my dinner party, and with anyone else brandy-addled enough to suggest that I am violence-oriented rather than cultural. And therefore, that being that, I invite you now to read and enjoy the cultural stories in this volume.

—ALFRED HITCHCOCK

THE BABY

Jonathan Craig

It had to be tonight, Harry Cogan knew. He'd lost his nerve last night and the night before, but tomorrow would be Vince Miller's last day in the lab before Vince and Susan left for Europe, and so it had to be tonight.

He glanced across the wide lab to the bench where Vince was cleaning up after his last experiment, getting ready to call it a day. Everyone else in the Radiobiology Section of Barth & Embick, Research Consultants, had left hours ago, but he and Vince had worked late, as usual, and it was now almost seven.

Harry stilled the tiny tremor in his hands, dried the damp palms on the side of his knee-length lab coat, and got to his feet. The time had come; if he hesitated a few minutes longer, it would be too late.

"Don't forget to put the baby to bed," Vince said pleasantly as Harry passed him on his way to the lounge. "Tuck the little baby into its little bed and put it in its little house."

Harry smiled. "The baby's already in bed and asleep," he said. It was a ritual, a standing reminder and reply that had been used in the lab as long as Harry could remember. The baby was a piece of radium half the size of an aspirin tablet; its bed was the small lead box in which it was kept; and its house was the lead-lined safe in which it and other radioactive materials were locked when not in use.

Just now, the baby was in its bed, but the bed itself was not in its house. It was in the right-hand pocket of Harry Cogan's trousers. It weighed two pounds, and felt like ten.

A very handsome man, Harry reflected as he entered the lounge. Too handsome. That was Vince Miller's big trouble. Too handsome and too brilliant. Before Vince had come to work there, Harry had been engaged to Susan, and heir apparent to the Chief of Section. Now, only seven months later, it was Vince Miller who was engaged to Susan, who was going to marry her next Saturday and leave with her for a honeymoon in Paris. And it was Vince Miller who had become Chief of Section.

Harry walked to the row of lockers against the far wall, trying not to think, not to feel. It was at this point that he'd had the failure of nerve last night and the night before; if he started thinking, started feeling, it might happen again. The chance of his being found out, he reminded himself, actually was almost nonexistent. Vince wouldn't notice any symptoms for at least two or three weeks, perhaps longer. By then, Vince and Susan would be in Paris, and there would be no reason for anyone to suspect that Vince's radium poisoning had been anything but accidental, the result of a risk recognized and assumed by all persons who worked with radioactive materials, as Vince and Harry did.

Once in Vince's clothing, next to his body, the baby would start him on a slow and horrible road to death. For radiogenic poisoning there was no antidote, no cure. By the time Vince had carried the baby home and back again, he would be doomed.

For Vince himself, Harry had no concern. No more concern than Vince had had for Harry when he stole his fiancée and his promotion. Harry had worked for two years to win Susan, and for eight years to win the promotion, only to have Vince deprive him of both in seven short months.

It was just too bad about Vince, Harry reflected as he took the small lead box from his pocket and opened it; just too bad. Trembling, he lifted the tiny wafer of radium from the box with forceps, and with his other hand opened Vince's locker. A moment later the baby was deep in the inside breast pocket of Vince's suit coat. No matter how many times Vince might reach into that pocket, the chance that his fingers would delve all the way to the bottom had to be reckoned in the thousands.

Harry closed the locker door soundlessly, wiped the sweat from his face with a paper towel, and walked back into the lab.

"Still working on that paper on radiothermics, Vince?" he asked as he crossed to his bench.

Vince nodded, pushed back his chair, and started for the lounge. "Still at it, Harry," he said. "Maybe I'll be able to finish it up tonight. I'm going to give it a good try, anyhow."

"Maybe it'll make you famous," Harry said.

Vince laughed. "Oh sure," he said. "Well, good night, Harry. See you in the morning."

Harry watched the broad back beneath the white lab coat disappear through the door, and then he sank down at his bench and sat very still, listening to the grate and clang of Vince's locker being opened and shut, and then the sound of Vince's footsteps fading rapidly down the long corridor that led to the street.

When Harry reached his apartment that night, he made a pitcher of martinis, put a Bartok album on the hi-fi, and sat down in the big leather chair Susan had given him for Christmas a year ago. A lot had happened this year, he thought. A lot more was going to happen before it was out.

Sipping his martini slowly, he tried for the hundredth time to discover any possible hitch, anything that could conceivably go wrong. But there was no possible hitch, nothing that could go wrong. True, Vince Miller might wear a different suit tomorrow. But that was no problem. Harry would be attending Vince's bachelor party tomorrow night at Vince's apartment, and with bachelor parties being what they were, finding an opportunity to visit Vince's closet and remove the baby from Vince's pocket would be simple indeed. Neither would the baby be missed tomorrow in the lab, because there was an identical baby in the next section, which Harry could "borrow" for the day.

Before the pitcher of martinis was half empty, Harry felt better than he had at any time since Vince Miller came to work at Barth & Embick. It wasn't the alcohol, he knew; it was the feeling that he had triumphed over Vince after all, that in a few short weeks, the promotion he deserved, and someday perhaps even Susan, would be his.

Half an hour later he felt an irresistible desire to call Vince up and talk with him. It would be good to sit here with his martini, knowing that Vince was doomed and that Vince didn't know it, making small talk with him while he enjoyed the secret wonder of having been the man who had doomed him. He smiled to himself, lifted the phone from the coffee table, and dialed Vince's number.

"Hello?" Vince's voice said.

"Harry, Vince."

"Oh, hello, Harry. What's up?"

"Nothing much. I was just sitting here thinking about you and Susan."

"Oh?"

"Yes. I just wanted you to know that there are no hard feelings."

"Because of Susan and me, you mean?"

"Yes. And the promotion, too, of course. I've written them off completely, Vince. The best man won, and I'm the first to admit it."

Vince laughed, a little uncertainly. "That's good to know, Harry," he said. "You'd already told me as much, but I'm glad to hear you say so again, just the same." He paused. "Was there anything else, Harry?"

"Only that I want to wish you and Susan all the luck in the world. I mean it, Vince."

"Well, thanks, Harry. Are you . . . sure there wasn't anything else?"

"No, nothing else," Harry said. "Just felt like giving you a call, that's all."

"Glad you did," Vince said. "See you tomorrow, then?"

"Right," Harry said. "Good night, Vince." He hung up, sat smiling down at the phone in his lap for a long moment, and then put it back on the coffee table. Tomorrow, he thought. Tomorrow. For seven months he'd dreaded each tomorrow. Now, he could scarcely wait for tomorrow to come.

When, finally, tomorrow came, and Harry walked into the lounge, he found he had the place entirely to himself. It was unusual for this time of morning, and he lost no time in making the most of it. Even before he exchanged his suit jacket for one of the white lab coats, he opened Vince Miller's locker, smiled when he saw that the suit coat hanging there was the same one Vince had worn yesterday, and reached down into the inside breast pocket for the baby.

It wasn't there.

Harry swore softly, probing hard into first one corner and then the other.

"Looking for something, Harry?" Vince Miller's voice asked from the doorway.

Harry felt something cold surge up through his body. It took all his strength to turn toward Vince, and when he spoke, his voice sounded like a stranger's.

"I was looking for a match," he said, forcing a grin he knew was as sickly as his lie. "I seem to have misplaced my lighter."

Vince nodded, reached into his pocket, and handed Harry a folder of matches. He laughed. "Now if you only had a cigarette, you could have yourself a smoke."

Harry laughed, too. In his ears, it sounded like a death rattle. He took the pack from his shirt pocket, fumbled a cigarette to his mouth, and glanced at Vince. "Care for one, Vince? They're your own brand."

"No, thanks," Vince said, smiling. "I guess that's what happened last night," he said. "I mean, you must have been looking for matches then, too."

Harry made two attempts to light his cigarette, failed both times, and finally put both the cigarette and the folder of matches in his pocket. "Last night?" he said.

"Yes. While you were out here in the lounge, just before I went home. I had to put something in the safe, and I noticed the baby wasn't there. You'd just got through telling me you'd put it to bed, so I thought I'd better call it to your attention."

"You mean you came . . . ?" Harry began. "You came out here in the lounge, Vince?"

"Well, not quite *in* the lounge," Vince said, smiling. "I got only as far as the door. And then . . . I don't know, I guess marrying Susan and going to Paris and all has sort of put me in a fog lately, Harry. Anyhow, I got as far as the door, and then suddenly, for *some* reason, I forgot about mentioning the baby to you." His smile widened. "Odd, wasn't it?"

Slowly, his eyes fixed unblinkingly on Vince's face, Harry sank down on the bench in front of the row of lockers.

"You look a little pale, Harry," Vince said. "Is it the baby you're concerned about? Listen, don't let it worry you. "It'll turn up, all right—probably in the last place you would expect to find it." He stood smiling down at Harry, his lips pursed, whistling almost soundlessly.

As Harry stared up at Vince in mounting horror, and his hand strayed involuntarily toward his inside jacket pocket, he could almost see the way Vince's face must have looked as he stood at the door of the lounge and watched the baby being placed in his coat. And then later, on his way out, Vince had merely switched the baby from his own pocket to Harry's.

Vince walked to the door, then paused, and turned back toward Harry. "I appreciated your calling me last night, old man," he said. "It's good to know there aren't any hard feelings."

Harry tried to take his eyes from Vince's face, but he could not. He ran his tongue across his upper lip. It was dry and numb.

"I'll drop you a card from Paris," Vince said, turning toward the door again. "And you must write me, too, Harry. Just a line or so—to let me know how you're feeling."

DON'T LIVE IN A COFFIN

Helen Nielsen

He grew more sinister by the moment. At first, he had been only a huge, shaggy man, ill-formed and gauche; but now he was someone Veda feared and dreaded. But she couldn't move away. That was the strange thing. She had to sit there beside the bowl of red roses and watch while he continued to daub paint on the canvas. Now and then, he would look up from it to her and a peculiar, penetrating warmth would rise up within her, as if her body was aware of some danger her mind had yet to identify. His eyes were dark and intense. When they so much as glanced at her, she couldn't move.

And all of the time she could see the sketch that had fallen to the floor beneath the easel: the sketch of a face with a red gash painted across its throat. . . .

When they met at lunch on Wednesday—Veda and Elaine always lunched together on Wednesday—Elaine was as enthused as ever. She had been enthused for the twenty-two years of their friendship, and such ebullience could become tiring. But it was spontaneous and uncontrollable, and a one-sided conversation had been flowing from the moment Elaine, late as usual, reached the table. Tardiness annoyed Veda. A professional woman had to learn punctuality. Elaine had never had to learn anything, as her conversation showed.

"I've found the most divine hairdresser! Honestly, Veda, you really must try him. Not that your hair doesn't look lovely as it is, but it's so severe and settled-looking. Henri—he spells it with an 'i' and pronounces it 'On-ree'—French you know—calls this 'April Zephyr.' What do you think?"

Elaine turned her head grandly. Currently, her hair was a honey-tone blonde, brushed forward and up with wisps of curls framing her forehead and almost hiding the fantastic little hat perched on the back of her crown.

"Very nice," Veda conceded. "What happens in May?"

"Oh, you—" And then Elaine smiled. "I wonder," she mused. "I'll have to wait and see. But if you'll just come down one day, Veda, I'll try to get Henri to take care of you. I'll have to make the appointment myself—he's that popular. He just doesn't take everyone."

"I'm flattered," Veda said, "but I can't see myself driving all the way to La Jolla just to have my hair done."

"Just to have your hair done!" The unhallowed thought was enough to make Elaine choke on her Chef's Low Calorie Delight. "And what could be more important, I'd like to know? Veda, are you just going to be a spectator for the rest of your life?"

Veda was learning now to listen to Elaine. It was an art. A surface part of her mind heard and answered, but the rest of it was free for more important things. Wednesdays were becoming tedious, particularly during Elaine's weekly lecture on poise, personality, and the character reformation of Veda Richards—now spurred by the opportune appearance of a waiter to take away the empty plates and deposit before Veda a smaller plate holding a silver pudding dish. This, Elaine observed with horror.

"Not prune whip!" she protested, as the waiter left. "Veda, I beg you—think before you pick up that spoon!"

Veda obediently observed a few seconds of immobile silence. "There, I've thought," she announced, and took up the spoon, tasted the pudding and nodded appreciatively. "Delicious!" she announced. "Are you sure you won't have some?"

"I can't look," Elaine groaned. "It's suicidal. It's a self-destructive impulse. Don't you realize what you're doing? You're giving up!"

"Elaine—please. Not that again."

"Yes, that again and again and again! You're a young woman, Veda, and an attractive one if you want to be. I know how much you loved Ken, but it's four years since the accident. Four whole years!"

"And two months," Veda added quietly.

"There, you see! You even count the months. That's not healthy, Veda. Look at me. I loved Peter madly; but when the louse left me, I started looking for another man the day I walked out of the divorce court. I haven't got one yet, but the decree isn't final for two weeks. You can't go on being a bereft widow forever. You should start seeing other men."

Veda smiled tolerantly. "Elaine," she said, "I see men every day of my life. A realty office isn't a cloister, you know."

"*Ken's* realty office," Elaine emphasized, "to which you have married yourself since he died. And you needn't, I know that. Ken left insurance and the house."

"Elaine, I asked you—"

"Why do you do it, Veda? Why do you bury yourself in that business? Why are you afraid to start living again?"

Elaine was shocked by her own frankness. She fell silent. Only one thing could stop a conversation so abruptly, and that was truth.

Veda looked up, smiling.

"Let's drop it for this week, shall we? Now, tell me. What else have you been doing that's interesting?"

Veda didn't really care, but it was a way of changing the subject. Elaine scowled her disappointment, and then returned to her natural brightness.

"Oh, this will interest you. I'm having my portrait painted."

It was just the sort of ridiculous thing Elaine would do. The thought crossed Veda's mind, but not her lips.

Vaguely, she asked, "In oils?"

"In oils. And by a wonderful artist—just wonderful! Wait—and I think I have some of the preliminary sketches right here in my handbag."

Elaine's handbags were voluminous. She required more equipment to go from place to place than anything short of an African safari. From deep within the folds of a huge patent-leather envelope, she now extracted several sheets of an artist's sketch pad which she proceeded to pass across the prune whip. Veda took them and held them before her. Simple sketches—crude, but sure. Sure, strong, and almost—and this was strange considering the subject—almost violent. And yet, they were unmistakably Elaine.

"He's good, isn't he?" Elaine asked.

Elaine was never really sure about anything.

"Yes," Veda said. "Quite good."

"And these are only sketches. You should see what he does in oils."

"Is he"—Veda hesitated over the word—"young?"

"Michael. Oh, no. He has gray hair."

Veda lowered the sketches.

"Then he's old."

"No, he's—oh, about our age, I imagine. His hair isn't really gray—just touches. Veda, why don't you try a bleach?"

Veda laughed. "Elaine, you're incorrigible. I merely asked his age because—" She held to her words for a moment. Why had she asked? The obvious reason was the easiest to face. "There's such strength in his work," she said.

Elaine glanced at her watch. "I'll tell Michael what you said—he'll appreciate it. But, Veda, if we're going to reach the theatre in time for the matinee, we'll have to get started *right now!*"

"Michael," Veda repeated, still staring at the sketches. "Michael what?"

"I do so hate to arrive late at a matinee. It's so awful climbing over all those women." And then Elaine seemed to hear Veda's question by some obscure route. "Hardin," she said. "His name is Michael Hardin. Do come along, dear. You shouldn't finish that prune whip anyway."

Elaine was already on her feet. There was nothing to do but hand her the sketches and follow.

That should have been the last of Michael Hardin. It was late when Veda returned home. The sun had gone down, and the day was making a final colorful flourish before darkness. She left her car in the garage and climbed the steps to find a freckle-faced twelve-year-old in sneakers and dungarees.

"You said for me to collect for the paper on Wednesdays—"

Veda put her key in the lock. "Yes, Jerry, I know I did. I was held up in traffic."

"Did you see a good show?"

"Show?" The door was unlocked. It swung inward. Veda stepped inside, then turned back, frowning.

"You said last week that you were going to some kind of a show."

"Oh, that—" Veda opened her purse. The boy was becoming a nuisance with his questions. "Let's see, now. I owe you $1.25—"

When the boy failed to respond, she looked up to find him staring beyond her. Across the living room, directly opposite the front door, a pair of glass doors opened onto the patio which overlooked the city below. Now the view was a deep golden panorama with the surrounding hills etched in mauve and purple. Jerry stared at it with all the inarticulate awe of a twelve-year-old discovering beauty.

"Golly," he said. "It's like a painting, only it's real!"

Veda smiled as her gaze followed Jerry's. There was a look of pride in her eyes.

"It really is," she said. "My husband planned it that way. He was a very clever man, Jerry. He said that whenever he came home at night after a hard day's work, he wanted to see the world at his feet instead of on his neck as it had been all day."

"I guess that's why you stay here, then," Jerry said. "I mean, you in this big house alone. People talk about it."

Tension returned to Veda's face. She counted out the money in the boy's hand.

"Thanks," he said, and started to turn away, but Veda's voice stopped him.

"What do people say about me?"

"Oh, things," Jerry answered, "—like what a nice-looking lady you are, and why do you live here all alone, like I said. Some of them say you'd be better off selling this house, and others say you'd be better off getting another guy to live here with you so you wouldn't be alone so much. Just things. But I know what you really need."

"What's that, Jerry?"

"A swimming pool out on the patio so all the kids around here wouldn't have to go to the park."

"And what of my carpets?"

"We'd come up the back way over the rocks. . . . Okay until next Wednesday, Mrs. Richards?"

"Okay, Jerry," Veda said.

When the door closed behind Jerry, Veda walked across the living room to the glass doors and stood staring out at the view. Light faded quickly at this time of evening, and she liked to watch the spectacle of the city being enveloped by the night. For years, she and Ken had done this together, sharing a cocktail and silence. Words were superfluous with Ken. Understanding had been there without them. She turned her head. From the glass doors, she could see Ken's portrait over the mantel. The light was failing fast, but his strong jaw and firm mouth were visible. He was still the master of the house, and it gave her a sense of security to know that he was there. The sort of talk the newsboy brought into the house annoyed her, and then, quite sharply, she remembered Elaine's words—

"Why are you afraid to start living again?"

Veda turned away from the windows. It was dark enough now to make the huge room a vault of shadows, but she didn't bother with the lights as she went up the stairs. At the top landing she paused, out of habit, to glance at Ken's door, and then turned into her own room. She snapped on the light and let her shadowy mood perish. It was nothing but the usual Wednesday letdown after Elaine's weekly missionary work; and, if the job she was doing didn't stop soon, the lunches would. There was a quick way to throw off the effects. She got out of her clothes and into a chenille robe; and then repaired to the bathroom, where she proceeded to fill the lavatory basin with hot water, and to take a bottle of shampoo from the medicine chest.

"All right, Henri," she announced to the mirror, "do your stuff!"

She'd no more than doused her head with shampoo when the telephone rang. Dripping, she clawed the towel rack and then raced for the bedroom. She threw herself across the bed and caught the call on the fourth ring. It was Elaine, bubbling as usual.

"Veda—I've got news!"

"Not a wreck, I hope," Veda said.

"Don't be silly! I've been home for nearly an hour. Michael dropped by to see if I could pose for him tomorrow, and I told him what you said about his work being so virile."

"I said that the drawing was strong, and that it was good," Veda corrected. "I didn't say 'virile.' You quoted me inaccurately."

Elaine giggled. "Well, it's all the same thing, isn't it? I mean, strength is strength. Anyway, he wanted to know who you were, and so I told him all about you. I even got out some old snapshots we took the year you and Ken and Pete and I vacationed at Ensenada, and—well, to make a short story shorter, Michael wants to paint you!"

Elaine made the announcement sound like an engraved invitation on the grand opening of Paradise. At the moment, it seemed something less.

"Of course he wants to paint me," Veda answered. "That's his profession. I'll wager he finds a photograph of someone he wants to paint in the home of every customer he gets. It's much cheaper than advertising."

There was a small but distinctly audible gasp from the other end of the wire; and then, unexpectedly, a man's voice saying—

"What an excellent idea, Mrs. Richards. I'm sorry I wasn't clever enough to have thought of it myself. This is Michael Hardin speaking."

Michael Hardin. Elaine should have warned her.

"He's on the extension," Elaine broke in.

"That's a dirty trick," Veda protested.

Michael laughed. "I think it's charming. And your idea is really a good one, but it's not the reason I asked Elaine to call you. I would like very much to paint you, Mrs. Richards. Your face has such interesting angles, and I like your mouth. And now"—he paused thoughtfully—"and I admire your frankness. What do you say, Mrs. Richards?"

"I have so little free time—"

"You take off Wednesdays—Elaine told me that. All I need is one day for a preliminary. Then you can decide if we are to go on with it."

It was time to say no—and firmly. But she had already insulted the man once.

"I don't know—" Veda began.

"But you do know," Elaine cut in. "Be a sport, Veda. Michael and I have it all planned. We'll drive in together on Wednesday morning and come directly to your house. Maybe you'll let me fix up something in your kitchen while you and Michael work. I'm getting awfully tired of those restaurants anyway."

Elaine was up to something. The call was too casual to be really casual. Veda felt a twinge of apprehension and then agreed.

"Wonderful," Elaine cried. "See you Wednesday."

And then the masculine voice, soft and penetrating.

"Good night, Mrs. Richards," Michael Hardin said.

Good night, Mrs. Richards. The words lingered in the room long after Veda had put down the phone. She returned to the bathroom and stared at the mirror. Her hair was short, and when she removed the towel, the front was almost dry. It fell in soft curls about her forehead. She pushed them up, forming a feathery frame similar to Elaine's.

And then Veda returned to her senses. "He only wants to sell a painting," she said aloud. Then she grabbed a brush and worked furiously to straighten out the curls.

Wednesday was a day of indulgences. Veda usually slept until nine, when sleep automatically died under the cutting knives of the gardener's lawn mower; but on the Wednesday following Elaine's call, sleep ended much earlier. Veda awakened with a sense of dread which her drowsy mind struggled to identify. She raised up from the pillows and glanced at the bedside table. Across the calendar of the day's appointments was written one name: Michael Hardin. Now the dread had an identity. She leaned back against the pillows, angry with herself for having allowed this intrusion on her privacy. It was more of Elaine's nonsense —and the last. And then Veda realized there was no need to see Michael Hardin at all. She had merely to pick up the telephone—

It rang before she could touch it.

"Mrs. Richards?" She recognized the voice at once. Only one voice had ever sounded that way. "This is Michael Hardin. I'm afraid I have some bad news."

He wasn't coming. Veda's hand tightened on the telephone.

"It's your friend, Mrs. Davis—"

"Elaine?"

"Yes, Elaine. A legal matter has come up and she won't be able to come with me today. I hope it doesn't make any difference."

It did make a difference. It sounded false.

"A legal matter," Veda echoed. "What sort of legal matter?"

"Oh, something about the final decree of her divorce, I think," Hardin answered. "A nuisance, but it needn't change anything. We can work better without her, and you needn't bother about lunch. I'll pick up something on the way."

"Oh, it's no bother, but—"

"Yes?"

"—the house is very difficult to find."

"Oh, Mrs. Davis told me all about that last night. After her directions, I could find it with my eyes closed."

"Last night?" It was time to say no, and firmly. This was one of Elaine's tricks. But there was no time. The telephone clicked and the connection was cut. Michael Hardin was coming. . . .

It was exactly noon when he arrived. Veda stood in the open doorway, a forced smile of greeting fading from her face. Michael Hardin. She'd seen a bold sketch and heard a warm voice; but now she found herself facing a shaggy, crude man who seemed to have been dropped carelessly into his wrinkled tweed suit, his graying hair receding sharply from his forehead, his dark eyes large and intense beneath heavy brows. He looked more like a retired weight-lifter than an artist. This couldn't be Michael Hardin—and yet, under one tweed-encased arm he carried a folded easel and a framed canvas, and in the opposite hand, a wooden case of oils.

Even a second of hesitation can be too long. Michael Hardin's smile hardened.

"Mrs. Richards?" he asked. "Yes, I know the face. I hope mine hasn't shocked you too much. I am Michael Hardin."

He walked past her, rudely, into the living room, his eyes on the glass doors to the patio. Halfway across the room he stopped, distracted by the portrait above the mantel. He stared at it for some seconds.

"Your husband," he said.

Veda closed the door behind her and came slowly across the room, annoyed but intrigued.

"Yes," she said.

He continued to stare at the portrait.

"He was a cruel man," he said.

"My husband—cruel? Why, there was never a more considerate—"

"There's cruelty in his mouth," Hardin insisted, "and the mouth never lies. The eyes often, but never the mouth."

He turned and stared at her then, and a smile came into his eyes. "Never the mouth," he repeated. "But then, he's been dead for some years."

"Four years," Veda answered.

"Yes, Elaine told me."

He walked to the glass doors and stepped out on the patio. It was a wide arc of carefully laid used brick, beyond which spread the now neatly clipped lawn, a rim of colorful flower beds, and a purple clematis vine scaling the used brick wall which separated the property from the estate next door. The rest of the yard was open, overlooking the city view. Michael Hardin surveyed the surroundings, advanced to the center of the patio, turned about slowly, describing a complete circle, until he faced Veda, who now waited just outside the glass doors.

"I did have trouble finding the house," he admitted. "It's secluded up here. I don't suppose"—he glanced at the brick wall—"you ever hear your neighbors, or they ever hear you."

"It's a quiet neighborhood," Veda admitted.

"That's good. Noise is a distraction. I don't work well with distractions." He glanced about. "Such as a gardener—"

"My gardener was here early this morning," Veda explained. "He won't be back for another week."

"And the neighbor's gardener?"

"They have the same one I have. He did their work immediately after mine, and they won't disturb you because they're both in Palm Springs."

"Good. We can work out here in the sunlight."

He began immediately to set up his equipment. There was a small bald spot about the size of a silver dollar at the crown of his head. It glistened in the sunlight as he bent over his work, and Veda found her slightly stunned mind fascinated with it until he straightened, turned toward her, and peered at her with those intense, boring eyes.

"The dress is no good," he said. "Take it off."

"What—?" Veda gasped.

"The collar. I don't want anything with a collar. Now, I need a chair for you and something for my box—"

At the near corner of the patio, a white wrought-iron table and chairs were set for lunch. Hardin grabbed one of the chairs with a violent motion—then set it aside as his eyes caught on the white bowl of red roses in the center of the table. He scooped up the bowl and brought it in a sweeping motion close to Veda's face. "And these," he added. "I like red with your coloring. Do you have a red dress?"

"An evening dress," Veda admitted.

Michael Hardin stared at her, the bowl of roses in his hands.

"My dear Mrs. Richards," he declared, "my canvas and my brush have no watches. They don't know what time of day I paint. Put on the red dress."

It was an order, and it was rude.

"Mr. Hardin—" Veda began.

"The red dress."

"Mr. Hardin—we've had no lunch."

"I never eat lunch. I must work while the light is strong. Light fades, Mrs. Richards. Everything fades if we're not careful." He was staring at her when he spoke the words. Now he looked away from her, his eyes sweeping the surroundings. "Your husband must have been a very successful man. This is a big house for a woman to live in alone."

"Did Elaine tell you to say that?" Veda demanded.

Hardin smiled. "You told me to say it, Mrs. Richards."

"I told you—?"

"Last week on the telephone." Now he peered past her into the house. "An upstairs, a downstairs—" he mused. "Yes, a perfect place." Then his eyes found hers again. "And you're an intelligent woman, Mrs. Richards. I like intelligent women. Most men don't. Their egos won't permit them the competition. They prefer the gay, fuzzy-minded type. The ones who are always bubbling over."

"Elaine Davis?" Veda queried.

Michael Hardin still held the bowl of flowers in his hands. He frowned at them—then walked back and replaced them on the table. After that, he crossed to the easel and began to set up the canvas.

"Dear Elaine," he murmured.

Veda watched him. "I think I'm beginning to understand," she said. "You wore out your hospitality with Elaine, and you've come here expecting a renewal."

"I've come here to do a painting," he said.

"I've decided that I don't want a painting done, Mr. Hardin."

He appeared not to hear. He opened the paint case and took out a knife. The blade glistened in the sunlight. Then he began to pare the end of a charcoal pencil. Without looking up, he said, "The red dress."

Rudeness, arrogance, insolence. She'd had enough. She took a step toward him—then stopped. Something slipped out from behind the canvas and fell to the bricks beneath the easel. Michael Hardin didn't notice it, but Veda stood fascinated while he pared at the charcoal pencil. It was the sketch Elaine had shown her a week ago, but with a noticeable addition: an ugly streak of red across the throat.

"In the National Gallery in Florence," Michael Hardin said, "there are two extremely interesting statues. Did you visit the National Gallery on your honeymoon, Mrs. Richards?"

The afternoon sun was warm on the patio. He had removed his jacket and rolled up his sleeves. His arms were like the arms of a longshoreman, and he painted as if driven by a dynamo.

Veda sat in the wrought-iron chair wearing the red dress. It was an old dress, but smart. Ken had picked it out; he'd always chosen her things, and his taste was excellent. On the low-cut neckline, she wore a fine mosaic pin—black with one red rose. Ken had bought it in Florence on their honeymoon. Michael Hardin had recognized its origin—hence the conversation.

"I suppose we did," Veda said. "I don't really remember. It was ten years ago."

"And a honeymoon," Hardin added. He paused in his work to stare at her. There was a half smile on his lips, and she could feel the penetration of his eyes. "You wouldn't remember. But there are two statues of one man in this gallery. Fascinating statues. The Renaissance Florentines were great gamblers, Mrs. Richards. Did you know that? They also had a remarkable sense of humor. Now, if I were to make a bet with anyone, and the stakes were to be skinned alive if I lost—and I lost, do you imagine that I would be skinned alive? Of course not! But this gentleman of Florence made such a bet—and lost, and, well, there are two life-size statues in the gallery—before and after. Mrs. Richards. Have I forced you to hold that position too long? You look pale."

He was diabolical. After almost an hour, Veda still wasn't certain if he'd seen the sketch on the pavement under the easel. He might have wanted it to be there.

"Those were the great days," he continued. "If ever I were to be reincarnated, that would be my age. Can't you see me, Mrs. Richards? A dashing Florentine artist—celebrated, romantic. Living like a prince in my magnificent villa—"

He had a patch on his trousers just below the left knee. It wasn't noticeable unless one stared at him long enough. Nonetheless, it was a clumsy job, as if he'd done it himself.

"Recognized and respected," he added, "and not forced to flattering brainless, chattering women."

"You hate women, don't you?"

Hardin didn't answer. He continued to paint.

"Particularly, Elaine Davis."

He scowled at the painting, bending closer.

"What was the legal trouble, Mr. Hardin?"

"I'm afraid I don't understand legal matters, Mrs. Richards. It seems there's a divorce pending—"

"But what was the trouble?"

"Perhaps there was a technicality—isn't that the term lawyers use—technicality? Wasn't your husband a lawyer, Mrs. Richards?"

"A lawyer? Why, no. Why did you think that?"

"Lawyers make a great deal of money."

"Some of them," Veda admitted. "Not all. I suppose it's the same in that profession as in my husband's. He worked very hard for everything he earned. Now that he's gone, I work just as hard."

"Why, Mrs. Richards?" He sounded like Elaine. Then he smiled. "But that's the kind of question you would expect of a foolish painter, isn't it? I never work. I just play around with my paints like a child. I never studied. I never pored over anatomy books until I knew the human body as thoroughly as a surgeon. No, more thoroughly. A surgeon needs only know the structure and functions, but an artist must know the rhythm and the poetry. Did you know there is poetry in the sternohyoid muscle, Mrs. Richards? Here, I'll show you—"

He stepped forward quickly and placed his hand on her throat. Veda drew back. The bowl of red roses stood on a pedestal beside her. Her shoulder brushed the pedestal and the bowl fell and smashed against the bricks. It was the sound of the bowl breaking that pulled Hardin's fingers from her throat.

"What a pity," he said. "They'll wither." He stooped and picked up one rose, held it a moment and then snapped the stem with his fingers and let it fall. He walked back to the easel, stepping aside to avoid the sketch of Elaine. The gesture was too obvious to be accidental.

He was playing with her. The whole performance was his revenge for poverty. Veda's mind told her this. But her flesh still felt the press of his fingers on her throat, and her eyes still found the mutilated sketch.

She had to know.

"You promised me a rest," she said.

She didn't give him a chance to protest. She left the chair and hurried to the telephone in the living room. She could dial direct, but now she'd forgotten the number. She dialed the operator and asked her to ring Elaine. She waited through ten rings before reluctantly putting down the telephone. When she turned, Michael Hardin stood at her shoulder.

"You should have known she couldn't answer," he said.

He was insane. The shadows were lengthening. Beyond the curve of the patio, the city lay screened behind a haze of heat—vast, silent and far away. Now Veda was acutely aware of the remoteness. They were alone, as Hardin had wanted from the first. And he must be insane; his words were senseless.

"A cruel man," he said. "The mouth never lies."

He was talking about Ken. It was incredible. Ken, who had always been kind.

"So he designed the house himself," he said.

"No," Veda said. "We had an architect. Ken worked with him."

"What did you design?"

"I—?"

"Anything? Anything at all? Oh, I know the husbands of

the women I paint, Mrs. Richards, and I know the women. Hollow women, like mannikins. Adorned, draped, worn in public like bouttonieres. Their table manners are exquisite; their conversations bright and sparkling, but never, never brilliant. Their wit appropriately vapid and occasionally suggestive; their laughter forced and shrill—"

He was describing Elaine. She'd been on his mind all this time. And that sketch on the pavement—deliberately unnoticed and deliberately obvious.

"Thank you," Veda said.

He looked up, brightly.

"Not you, Mrs. Richards. You don't chatter or sparkle. You're a prisoner. You live in a coffin."

"A coffin—?"

"That's why I painted you in red. Red is the color of life. I must get you out of that coffin."

Hardin still stood in the sunlight. He was perspiring. Beads of sweat had gathered on his eyebrows and ran down the creases in his face. To Veda he seemed to grow more sinister by the moment—but she couldn't move away. That was the strange thing. She had to sit there and try to draw him out.

"I'm not aware of living in a coffin," she said.

"Most people aren't," he answered. "They clutter up their lives with appointments and schedules and luncheon dates. They keep busy, like a hoard of droning bees. The men make a great deal of money so they can buy wives, who wait patiently for them to die—"

"Mr. Hardin!"

"Aren't you glad he's dead?"

"No! I loved my husband!"

"Dutifully?"

"What?"

"Dutifully. You were trained to love your husband. From childhood up you were trained, the way you were trained in your ABC's and 2 plus 2 equals 4—"

"I don't know what you're talking about," she said, angrily.

"I'm talking about the reason you wanted me to come here," he answered.

"I wanted you—?"

"Didn't you, Mrs. Richards?"

She couldn't answer. She'd gone to the bathroom and

pushed up curls on her forehead after that first call. She'd
heard his "good night" clinging to the air. But that was
when he was only a voice. Now he was real. Now he was
threatening.

The house was a half dark vault behind her. She'd left
once to go to the telephone and he'd followed her. Suppose
she left now and went to the door, opened the door and
ran out into the street. Would he follow her again? It was
a good forty feet to the front door—through the glass
doors, through the living room, through the entry hall.
If she sat quietly, he might just continue to talk out his wild-
ness. But if she moved—

And then the doorbell rang. Hardin stopped painting.

"What was that?" he asked.

It rang again.

"Are you expecting anyone? No, I'll go—"

He tried to push past her, but Veda had started to her
feet with the first ring. She reached the door ahead of him,
pulled it open wide and found herself facing Jerry.

"Your paper, Mrs. Richards."

"Oh, Jerry," she said. "I'm so glad you rang the bell. I'll
get my purse and—"

"That was last week, Mrs. Richards."

"Last week?"

"You only pay once a month. I just wanted to leave the
paper. Hey, you're painting out there."

Jerry started to step into the room, his eyes fixed on the
patio beyond the doors. But Hardin's hand on his chest
pushed him back.

"We're working," he said firmly.

"I only wanted to see—"

"We have to work fast while the light holds."

"Okay, mister. Okay." Jerry gave Hardin one long,
penetrating stare, shrugged, and backed out of the door.
"See you next week, Mrs. Richards."

Hardin closed the door.

"I'll take the paper," he said.

It was a small, loose roll in her hands. She held it an
instant too long. He pulled it from her, roughly.

"The light," he said. "I'd better get to work."

There were different stages to any experience: shock,
fear, and, finally, anger. The shock of Hardin's rude en-

trance and the fear of his strangeness were giving way to the final stage.

"You're too tense," he said. "You must relax."

"I'm tired," Veda answered.

"Is that what the lines are?"

"Lines?"

"At your mouth—between your eyes. Oh, an artist's eyes are trained to see, Mrs. Richards. I see how busy you keep yourself—how fast you run. You must use sedatives to sleep."

"Occasionally."

"Frequently, I would say. More and more frequently. And you see fewer and fewer people."

"I work with people every day."

"But they irritate you, don't they?"

"I don't like being analyzed, Mr. Hardin."

"I have to paint what I see."

"Don't you see what you're looking for?"

Hardin looked up and smiled. "Touché!" he said.

"What's in your own mind," Veda added. "What's in your own eyes."

"She fights back," Hardin said. "Good. I knew red was her color."

"And in your own desire."

She had reached anger, and the spell she'd been under was broken. She came to her feet. Suddenly, she realized how afraid she had been, and now she wasn't afraid at all because now she understood. At first there had been doubts in her mind that Elaine would go to such lengths. But then came the realization that she was capable of anything —even this.

"And Elaine's desire," she said.

"Elaine's?"

"Wasn't this whole performance her idea? Even the too obvious sketch with the red paint smeared across the throat?"

He stopped painting. He put down his pallette and stared at her.

"And all of that delightful conversation about a skinned man, and that dramatic performance with your fingers on my throat. Even the telephone call that Elaine wouldn't answer. Weren't they all parts of your act?"

"Act?" he echoed.

"Overplayed, Mr. Hardin, and transparent. Elaine sent you here to taunt and insult me—my way of living, my house, my husband—"

"Who is so conveniently dead."

Veda stopped. Once before she had reached such a stop. One week ago at the luncheon table when Elaine had asked a question for which there was no answer.

"Why are you afraid to start living again?"

"No man is mourned so long unless he was thoroughly hated," Hardin added. "Hated so much that no one is allowed to take his place. You call it loyalty. But isn't loyalty to the dead a kind of disloyalty to life?"

"Elaine told you to say that!"

"A kind of noble selfishness, Mrs. Richards. A dead man makes no demands—"

He had his hands on her arms, but it wasn't his hands that held her. It was his words. They had seared like acid.

They stood close for one terrible moment.

"Mrs. Richards! Mrs. Richards!"

Veda pulled away.

"Hey, Mrs. Richards! See, I told you kids could come up over the rocks."

Incredibly, it was Jerry. He stood at the edge of the patio, dirt-smeared and panting very hard.

"I came"—he paused, staring at Hardin—"I came for the paper," he said.

"The paper—?"

"I think I got mixed up and left the early edition. I always leave you the latest edition, Mrs. Richards. If you'll just look across the top of the front page and see if there's a blue streak—"

Hardin had left the paper on the unused luncheon table. As Jerry moved toward it, he loosed his grip on her arms and shoved her toward the boy. He whirled about, paused for a moment, and then leaped over the side of the patio and went scrambling down the rocks. Someone shouted from below. Someone cried—"There he is! Get him!" Veda started to move toward the edge of the patio, but Jerry pulled her back.

"Those are the police," he said. "I went for them after I saw that guy and the painting stuff out here. You don't want to go down there. You might get shot, or something."

"Shot?" Veda echoed.

"It's in your paper, Mrs. Richards. All about this lady whose throat was cut—"

When Jerry opened up the paper, Veda saw what her imagination had refused to believe. Elaine's photograph and a headline: "Wealthy Divorcée Slain"

"There's a drawing of this artist guy inside," Jerry said. "She had him painting her picture. Last night the neighbors heard them talking real loud. He asked her to marry him, and she laughed at him. They found her this morning with her throat cut."

Veda's hand went to her own throat, but it was Hardin's fingers that she felt. And she'd thought it was all a trick of Elaine's to shock her out of the past. Her hand came down again and reached out for Jerry—for something warm, and young, and alive. But Jerry had moved over to a spot in front of the easel. He stood as though rooted.

"Golly!" he said.

She heard him, vaguely.

"Golly, what a painting!"

She walked to where Jerry stood. An artist's eye sees, Hardin had told her.

He had painted her in red—red to match the blood oozing from her throat—and above the throat a face remarkable in one terrible respect. It was a face that a mad artist might see; it was a face without a mouth.

A HUNDRED TIMES

Syd Hoff

Miss Compton was pretty; so much prettier than any other teacher in P.S. 189, or any other lady he had ever seen. That's all Philip could think of ever since the new term began.

"Philip, have you been listening to me?" she asked suddenly.

He felt his cheeks getting hot. "N-no, ma'am."

"Then you will please step to the blackboard and write a hundred times, 'I must pay attention in class.'"

Philip obeyed. He stood at the blackboard and wrote until the chalk in his hand almost disappeared, while the rest of the class went on with the arithmetic lesson.

When he was finished, Philip went back to his seat and continued looking at Miss Compton.

Only Allan Harbach, alongside him, knew how Philip felt. "Philip loves Miss Compton," he said in a low voice so nobody else could hear.

Philip reached over and punched him. What Allan said was true, but he didn't want to hear it, maybe because Allan made it sound like something quite dirty.

"Why did you do that?" Miss Compton asked, coming up the aisle. She was even pretty when she was angry.

Philip could only hang his head.

"It was a very nasty thing to do," the teacher said, observing the other boy's mouth bleeding. "Allan, why did Philip attack you?"

"I can't tell, Miss Compton. I can't tell on Philip because I'm no tattletale."

No wonder Philip returned to the blackboard, this time to write:

I must never strike Allan.

I must never strike Allan.

I must never . . .

When he got back to his seat this time, Allan whispered, "I'll get even with you, Philip. You'll see." He knew how to whisper so Miss Compton wouldn't catch him.

Not Philip. When he tried to whisper an apology, he wound up at the blackboard once more:

I must never talk in class.

I must never talk in class.

I must never . . .

And Allan? He became a monitor.

"Class, Allan is your monitor. He will stand at the top of the staircase and report any talking in line, or other infractions of the rules."

Philip tried to be careful on that staircase. He had a feeling the new monitor would try to make trouble for him.

He wasn't wrong:

I must never drop papers on the staircase. . . .

I must never whistle in line. . . .

I must never spit. . . .

Who had done any of those things? Not Philip. But it was easier to write on the blackboard than argue with Allan. And who wanted to make Miss Compton mad anyway?

"Listen, Allan, want this ballpoint pen? I've got two of them."

"Who needs your ballpoint pen?"

"How about my bike? You can ride it all afternoon."

"Keep your old bike."

"Hey, how about you and me having a catch? I've got a dandy new ball. A high bouncer."

"I wouldn't catch with you if you had the last ball in the world."

Philip was ready to give up. What else could he invite Allan to do after school?

"Here, take a punch at me, Allan, then we can be even."

Allan sneered and walked away.

Came the big test in math and Philip thought the other boy was willing to be friends after all. There was Allan turning his paper toward him, straight toward him! It was too much to resist, looking at that paper, so:

I must never cheat on a test.

I must never cheat on a test.

I must never . . .

It was inevitable that Miss Compton should send for one of Philip's parents.

"Perhaps I ought to go," said Philip's father.

"Nonsense," said his mother. "I'm sure no capital crime has been committed. What's the point in your taking time off from the office?"

Philip stood before the two women, thoroughly ashamed. "I'll try to do better," he promised. "I'll try."

"I've been having your son do a little writing on the blackboard whenever he does something naughty," said Miss Compton.

"Ah, yes, a hundred times," smiled Mrs. Gersten. "They used to do that in my day, too."

"Teaching's changed in many ways, but some of the old methods are still the best."

"I'm sure they are. I was only saying to my husband the other day . . ."

Later at home, Philip's mother said to him, "She's very pretty, your teacher."

"I know," he said, feeling himself blushing, and repeated what he had already promised. "I'll try to do better. I'll try."

It didn't do any good. He went on paying for the misdeeds Allan arranged for him, writing on the blackboard until his fingers hurt.

"The Board of Education provides us with plenty of chalk," Miss Compton said grimly.

I must never shout on the staircase . . .

I must never write on the walls any . . .

I must go down one step at a time . . .

I must not be in a hurry . . .

At least his rows were getting neater; he hoped she noticed.

One morning Philip arrived at school a little late and the staircase was empty, except for Allan standing waiting at the top of it, a big grin on his face.

"Destroying school property, huh?" he chuckled, grabbing the books from Philip's hand and tearing out pages as Philip tried to pass him.

The second bell hadn't rung yet, and there was too much noise in the building for anybody to hear.

"You're tardy," Miss Compton started to say when

Philip entered the room, but the boy walked directly to the blackboard.

He picked up a piece of chalk and started writing.

"Philip, go to your seat until I tell you to do that," said the teacher, then stopped as she saw the words in white forming on the black slate:

I must never push Allan down the staircase.
I must never push Allan down the staircase.
I must never push Allan down the staircase.
I must never . . .

He had written it almost a dozen times before she could bring herself to run out in the hall and look over the bannister, while the sound of the chalk screeched on and on in her ears.

WEEP FOR THE GUILTY

Henry Slesar

The truck from Edalia was due at eleven o'clock, but Johnny Bree didn't have a wristwatch to mark its approach. None of them were permitted watches; their hours were measured by the commands and whistles of the guards. But Johnny needed one now, on that hot, sundrenched morning, standing in the reddish-brown soil and looking toward the distant granary and the vanishing point of the road to Edalia.

He walked up behind Fisher, and the guard wheeled quickly. He relaxed when he saw who it was; Johnny was no trouble-maker. "What's up, Handsome?" he said.

"Stomach," Johnny said. He laced his fingers over the blue shirtfront and grimaced. "Got a cramp or something. Could I go in the shed and rest a while?"

Fisher's big, bland face looked doubtful. Then he said, "Sure, go ahead."

Johnny thanked him and went inside.

The shed was dark and cool, with a rich farm smell. Johnny went to the sink and doused his face with water. He looked at his dripping hands and saw they were trembling. He had mentally rehearsed this moment for weeks, but now he was nervous and afraid of failure.

Five minutes later, he heard the wheel hum of the approaching supply truck. Moving swiftly, he pushed a riding cultivator toward the darkest corner and made himself a hiding place. In another minute, the truck would brake to a halt outside, and the unloading process would begin. He had observed the operation for a month. When the crates were unloaded in the shed, the driver and his helper would spend a cigarette's time with Fisher or one of the others. That was when he had to make his play.

The truck had stopped, and the doors of the shed were opening. The two men did their job methodically. Finally, the last crate had been stacked. They shut the doors when they left.

Johnny waited, and then went to the doors. Encouraged by silence, he opened one an inch, and saw the back of the truck, open.

It was now or never.

He made the rear of the truck in three leaps of his long legs. He clambered inside, crawled on all fours to the dark end. There was a loose tarp lying in back, and he pulled the heavy, damp fabric over him.

Then a figure cut off the light from the rear doors, and a hand slammed them shut. He felt the truck sway as the two men climbed into the cab. He listened to the nagging sound of the ignition and prayed. When the engine turned over, he almost sobbed with relief. They were on their way.

At a point he estimated to be ten miles away from the farm, he kicked open the rear doors and watched the road sliding away from the wheels. He waited until the truck was going upgrade. Then he dove off, and tumbled into the grit.

Erika Lacy was in a mood only speed could satisfy. On the flat, empty stretch of highway between Sycamore Hills and town, she whipped the horsepower of her car, forgetting the admonition of her Uncle Bell. "Never drink or drive when you're angry," he had said, and Uncle Bell knew all about anger, he was the expert. He had set her a bad example, and Erika, thinking about Huey Brockton and their quarrel on the Point Placid dance floor the night before, had the same tight-mouthed expression she had seen so often on her uncle's face. With her reddish-gold hair flying in the convertible's air stream, she looked like a firecracker on the way to an explosion.

Uncle Bell himself had been the subject of the quarrel. Huey had a pointed dislike for Erika's guardian, and it was obvious where he had acquired the prejudice. His father, Howard Brockton, was Uncle Bell's business partner and chief antagonist, and their continuing feud had given Point Placid something interesting to talk about for the past three years.

Whoosh! The convertible swept by a column of roadside saplings and made them bow to its breeze. In the distance, a trailer truck was crossing the highway at Edalia Road, and she slowed down grudgingly. The action helped ease some of her tension. She thought about the lunch she was going to have with her Uncle Bell in town; he had promised to take her to the exclusive and masculine Iron Club, and she was looking forward to it. By the time she spotted the lonely, somewhat pathetic figure of the young man with the hooked thumb, she was feeling almost amiable. That was why she stopped, ignoring still another edict of Uncle Bell's: *Never pick up a hitchhiker.*

"Going to town?"

He was limping as he came forward, and trying to smile through a dust-caked face. He wore faded blue coveralls.

"Yes," she said. Then, with a sudden pang of doubt, added: "What are you doing way out here?"

"Car broke down," he grinned, opening the door.

He climbed in beside her, and Erika made a quick appraisal before driving off. He was a good-looking young man with a crooked grin that wasn't self-conscious, and he had the ruddy brown glow of the outdoor worker.

"Must have been a hot walk," she said cheerfully. "We can stop at a gas station to see about your car, and you can get something to drink."

"Don't want to see about the car," he laughed.

"What?"

"I'm abandoning the old heap. Let the crows have it, I don't ever want to see that pile of bolts again."

Erika laughed, too. "I've got some sour balls in the glove compartment. Maybe they'll keep you going a while."

"Thanks," he said, punching the button on the compartment door. "I thought I was going to have to walk all the way into town. Just quit a job over in Delmar, thought I'd go to Point Placid and see if I could do better."

"Farmer?"

"Not any more," he said fervently. "Not any more." He unscrewed the cap on the candy jar, and held it toward her. "Want one?" he said.

She was about to answer no when she felt the sudden, startling jab of the metallic point in her ribs. She stiffened, and almost let go of the wheel.

"Easy," the young man said. "This isn't very sharp but it can hurt. Just pull up to the side and keep quiet and you won't get hurt."

"What is this?" she said angrily.

"I said pull over, Miss. I wouldn't want to hurt you, you've been nice." He increased the pressure of his argument, and Erika, her eyes stinging with tears, put her foot on the brake and eased the convertible to a halt. When the car stopped, she looked down to see that his weapon was a small screwdriver, taken from the glove compartment.

She said: "This is a nice way to return a favor."

"Get out of the car, Miss."

"I won't!"

"I'll probably kill you if you don't."

She faced him, and he seemed as calm as ever. That frightened her, his calmness, and she decided it was safer outside the car. She stepped out, waiting for his next command.

"Throw that purse over."

She tossed it into the car. "You won't find much in it," she said contemptuously.

He slid under the wheel, and put the purse on the other side of him. Then he released the parking brake, and stomped the accelerator. The convertible zoomed away, kicking up dust.

"You—stinker!" Erika shouted after him. Then she started to cry. When a healthy sense of indignation returned, she stopped crying and tried to think. It was another eight miles into Point Placid, and her chances of getting a lift on the deserted stretch of highway were small. She began to walk.

Five minutes later, she realized that her spike heels were no help on the hard-baked road. She took off her shoes, and began a barefoot march toward civilization, cursing herself for forgetting Uncle Bell's good advice.

In the distance, she saw a promising puff of dust. It was a car, heading in the wrong direction, but she stepped into the middle of the road and began to wave frantically. When it was a hundred yards away, she saw that she was flagging her own convertible.

It drove past her a few feet; then the young man in the blue coveralls swung the wheel sharply and made a U-turn. He cut the engine, and leaned over the door.

"I'm sorry," he said.

She hobbled across the road. He got out of the car on the far side and just waited, hangdog.

"I said I'm sorry," he repeated. "I don't know what made me do that, I must have been crazy with the heat."

She put her shoes on, and then climbed behind the wheel. She didn't touch the pedal. "I don't get it," she said flatly.

"There's nothing to get. I'm no thief, I just made a mistake. I didn't touch anything in your purse. You want to check?"

She chewed her lip. "I trust you."

"You don't have any reason."

"You came back," Erika said. "I guess that's reason enough." She turned her head and glared at him. "Well, get in. You won't enjoy walking; I know I didn't."

"You mean that?"

She put the car into gear. Quickly, the young man opened the right-hand door and climbed in beside her."

"My name is Johnny Brennan," he said.

She knew he wanted to talk, and that her silence would be the best incentive. More than that, Erika knew she wanted to listen.

"I've never done anything like this before," he said. "When that old jalopy of mine broke down, I guess it was the last straw. All I could think about was getting away someplace, anywhere, doing something different."

"When I quit that job over in Delmar, I swore I'd never work a farm again. I've got brains. You can't think on a farm, you're just another animal—"

"There are college graduates on farms these days."

He laughed bitterly. "Not the kind I work. Dirt farmers, pig farmers. I want to wear a white shirt for a change. Only who'd hire me? They smell hay on me the minute I walk into a place. And it's all because of the war . . ."

"The war?"

"You probably don't even know what war I'm talking about; it's that mess we had over in Korea. I joined the Army when I was sixteen, lying about my age just to get away from home. I was over on Heartbreak Ridge when I was eighteen. I was just a dumb kid. I didn't know what it was all about. I ended up getting shot to pieces."

"I'm sorry," Erika said quietly.

"I wasn't too bad off; a hospital was a better place than a battlefield, only it was a long war for me. It took them eight years to put me together again. At that, I did better than Humpty-Dumpty.

"By the time they let me go, I was pale and skinny and in need of exercise. The Army doctors recommended outdoor work; they got me my first farm job. Since then, I've been trying to get away from it. Do you know what I'm talking about?"

"I guess so," Erika said. "I don't agree with you, maybe, but I can see how you feel. My grandfather was a farmer, but my uncle, my father's brother, he always hated the life. He ran away from the farm when he was eighteen years old."

"How did he do?"

"He did all right. He owns the Lacy Machine Company in Point Placid; he and his partner, anyway."

Johnny whistled.

"That's where I was going before you stopped me," Erika said. "To meet my Uncle Bell for lunch. Before you made your debut as a bandit." She smiled. "That's one profession I'm afraid you won't succed at."

"I know what you mean," Johnny grinned. "Of course, if I'd known you were an heiress, I might have been tougher. Bet you've got a million bucks in that purse."

"That's what you think. I've got exactly thirty dollars."

"Well, that's thirty bucks more than I've got. When I left Delmar, I didn't even wait for my back wages. I don't even own a decent suit of clothes."

Erika gave him a sidelong glance and did something impulsive. She picked up the purse and dropped it into his lap.

"Open it," she said. "Take the money."

"No," Johnny said firmly. "I didn't mean you to take it that way. If I wanted your dough, I could have stolen it."

"I want you to have it," Erika said. "You'll need a suit of clothes if you're looking for a job."

"I wouldn't even know where to look."

Erika hesitated.

"I know one place," she said. "I've got an in with the boss. I don't know what kind of job it would be, maybe even sweeping floors. But I could put in a good word for you."

Ahead of them, glinting in the sun, was the tower of the Point Placid Hotel, surrounded by the smaller structures of factories and office buildings. Johnny stared toward the low skyline before answering.

"You mean your uncle?" he said. "You'd do that for me?"

"He's usually pretty agreeable when he's eating," she said lightly. "Won't be any harm in asking. Go on, take the money. Buy a gray suit; it's Uncle Bell's favorite color. I'll tell him that you'll be dropping around the front office at three o'clock; he'll be expecting you."

"This is nuts. You don't owe me anything."

"No, but you'll owe me thirty dollars. I'll expect it back, once you're working." She laughed. "The address is 300 Main Street. And you better be on time. Uncle Bell's a bug on punctuality. And a few other things."

Johnny Brennan looked at the purse, and frowned. Then he opened it.

The Lacy Machine Company was at the end of Main Street, and its boundaries were marked by a high wire fence and several pugnacious men in uniform. The plant itself was spread out like a game of dominoes, with half a dozen one-story buildings jutting out at right angles toward each other. Johnny, walking up to the main gate in a poorly fitting suit that had cost twenty dollars of Erika's thirty, peered through the wire mesh at the sprawling factory and decided that Uncle Bell was doing very well indeed.

He ran a gauntlet of gate guards, receptionists, and secretaries, and finally the mahogany door of Beldon Lacy's office. He knocked, and a gruff voice told him to come in.

He had expected something lavish, but found only size and clutter. There were two large desks, one used as a repository for papers and debris; the other faced the window and was almost as disordered. Behind it was a high-backed swivel chair, and the head denting the leather cushion was striking in its ferocity. It was the face of a warrior and the impression didn't disappear when Bell Lacy stood up and revealed the ordinary striped tie and dull gray suit of the businessman. Under a high forehead, his eyebrows overhung dark sockets; a big nose was complemented by a jutting chin; there were small scars on both cheeks. Johnny had a hard time relating Erika Lacy's sweet mouth and incandescent eyes to her uncle's features.

"I'm Johnny Brennan," he said shyly. "I was told to be here."

Lacy wiped a hand quickly across his mouth.

"Yes, sure," he said. "Erika told me about you. Shut that door, will you? Place is full of drafts."

"Yes, sir." He shut the door quietly.

"Come on over here," Lacy said, coming around the front of the desk. He was grinning oddly.

Johnny walked up to him. Lacy put both fists on his hips and looked him over. The grin tightened.

"So you're Johnny, huh?"

"Yes, sir."

Lacy didn't hurry. He pulled back his right arm, and Johnny had plenty of time to see the hard ball of his fist looming up like a rock. When it landed on the side of his jaw, he was knocked halfway back to the wall. He stumbled over his own feet, and when he tried to get up, he couldn't tell wall from ceiling.

Lacy's hand came toward him, and he flinched, but it was being offered in aid. Johnny hesitated, and then accepted. He was pulled to his feet, and Lacy said:

"That was for what you did to my niece. Now if you still want to talk about a job—have a seat."

Johnny looked at the face. There was neither hostility nor apology in it.

"Okay," he said numbly.

Looking back on the interview, Johnny couldn't recall much of it. His jaw was aching, and the machine-gun questions rattling out of Beldon Lacy's mouth were almost too fast to duck.

"How old are you?"

"Twenty-eight."

"Parents alive?"

"Don't know."

"Don't *know?*"

"I mean—yes. I think so."

"Ever do anything but farm jobs?"

"I worked in a gas station for about a month."

"Mechanic?"

"No, sir. Just cleaning up, filling tanks."

"Can you run a lathe, a drill press?"

"No."

"Clerical work? Typing? Do filing?"

"I'm not much good at it."

"What *can* you do?"

Johnny rubbed his aching face.

"There's a dispensary on the second floor," Lacy said sourly. "Stop in there on your way out and get some court plaster on that bruise. Don't tell 'em where you got it. I got a bad enough reputation around here as it is."

"I wasn't going to tell them."

"You deserve a lot worse. I could report you to the police for what you did." He stood up, scowling. "This is probably the dumbest thing I've ever done," he said. "And I've done plenty. I'm going to fix you up with a job in the Supply Department. You'll work for an old geezer named Gabriel, he runs the place. You'll help him take care of the tool room and see that the men get the stuff they need. The pay is sixty bucks a week. You want it or not?"

Johnny swallowed hard. "Yes," he said. "I want it."

"I'll expect you to keep an extra clean nose around here. Erika thinks you're some kind of hero, all because you changed your mind about robbing her. That doesn't rate with me."

"I guessed that," Johnny said, moving his jaw.

Lacy laughed suddenly.

"It wasn't a bad right cross, was it? I used to do some pro boxing when I was twenty. In those days, a ring record was like a Phi Beta Kappa key. My first boss at the iron works hired me because he liked my style. Business was a lot rougher in those days. And a lot better," he added bitterly. "Okay, that's all. Report to this building on Monday morning, nine o'clock."

"All right," Johnny said.

"You'll like it here," Lacy sneered. "It's a real nursery school. You'll get free hospitalization, time and a half for overtime, bonuses, pensions. You'll even get a free physical; that's for group insurance. We do everything but wipe your nose for you."

"Nobody has to wipe my nose."

"Payday is next Friday. Got anything to live on now?"

"Not much."

Lacy took out his wallet and peeled off two tens. "That's an advance," he said. "We'll bite it off your first check."

"Thanks," Johnny said.

He walked out of the administration building without making the turn toward the dispensary. He spent the rest of the afternoon in an idle stroll around town. At six, he saw a sign in a brownstone window that read: ROOMS. He inquired, and the cheapest was a one-room rear that rented for nine dollars a week, payable in advance.

He borrowed a stamp, writing paper, and an envelope from the landlady, and put a dollar bill inside. Then he checked the phone directory for Erika Lacy's address. He found it listed beneath Beldon Lacy's name: RFD 1, Sycamore Hills. Then he wrote a note.

Dear Heiress, it read. *This is the first installment. I now owe you twenty-nine dollars and thanks.*

Johnny

P.S. I'm working. Can I see you sometime? How about Saturday?

As she came up the driveway to the stone house on the hillside, Erika saw her Uncle Bell's car parked in the garage. Beldon Lacy rarely came home from the factory on week nights, preferring to spend them in his spartan room at the Iron Club. When he did show up, it was usually under the impetus of a black mood.

She found him in the living room, with an unopened bottle of whisky and an empty glass.

"Hi," she said, trying to smile. "What happened? Club throw you out for not paying your bar bill?"

"Just felt like coming home."

She took the seat opposite and studied him. "I know you better than that. Something's bothering you. Is it Brockton?"

"Isn't it always Brockton? Only this time things have come to a head."

"What's he done?"

"It's not what he's done. It's what he plans to do. He came into my office today and asked me to reconsider his offer. I told him I wouldn't sell my interest for a million bucks, just like I always told him. That didn't shut him up."

"He can't *force* you to sell—"

"Can't he? You don't know Brockton. He can't tell a bit from a bushing, but he can do more tricks than Houdini." He picked up the whisky bottle and looked at the label.

"He's calling a special meeting of the stockholders. He's planning to make a proxy fight out of it."

"Fight? What do you mean?"

"He thinks he can get enough stockholder support to put me in the freezer for good. If he can't buy me out, he can push me out, me and my old-fashioned methods."

"It won't work," Erika said flatly. "The plant can't do without you, Uncle Bell. Even if Brockton doesn't realize it, the other stockholders will. You *built* the place."

"Don't underestimate him, Erika. That was the mistake I made three years ago. He knows how to cozen people, he talks dividends to them, capital gains, all that junk." He broke the seal on the bottle and poured himself a drink. "I don't mean to cry on your shoulder. I'll handle Brockton, don't worry. I've always been able to take care of myself." He downed the drink quickly, and then stood up. "Think I'll hit the sack early," he said.

She watched him move slowly to the door, hesitating before asking her next question. "Uncle Bell—"

"Yes?"

"Did Johnny Brennan start work today?"

He turned. "Yeah, bright-eyed and bushy-tailed. We put him through the wringer, and he'll start in the Supply Department tomorrow. I'll have to tell Gabe to keep an eye on him, see that he doesn't walk off with the petty cash."

"That's not fair," Erika said. "I told you about him, Uncle Bell, he's no thief."

"What makes you so sure?"

"Because no thief would have done what he did. I think you can trust him."

"Do you trust him?" he asked quizzically.

"Yes."

Her uncle frowned. "Didn't you tell me he was some kind of war hero? In Korea?"

"I didn't say he was a hero, only that he was shot up pretty bad. He was in an Army hospital for a long time."

"That's funny," he grunted. "On account of he passed his insurance physical with flying colors. Those Army doctors must have done quite a job."

Erika started. "No sign of a wound?"

"Not a mark on him, arms, legs, no place. That'll teach you to be so trusting, moppet. You don't know people the way I do." He looked dejected, and turned back to the doorway. He paused there a moment and said: "There's some mail for you. I left it on the hall table."

Alone in the living room, Erika tried not to think about Johnny Brennan, but thoughts of him kept intruding. She was glad for the interrupting sound of automobile tires on the gravel in the driveway.

She knew it was Huey Brockton even before she reached the front hall; the staccato sound of the buzzer was in his own playful rhythm. She didn't open the door, but leaned against it and said:

"Sorry, nobody home."

"Aw, come on, Erika."

"Go away, Huey, it's late."

"I've got to talk to you a minute. Please," he said pitifully. "It's freezing out here."

She couldn't stop the smile. She opened the door on the warm August night. Huey, wearing a silky sports shirt with tight-rolled sleeves, was hugging himself.

"Brr," he said. "Must be an early frost." He closed the door behind him and reached for her. She pulled away quickly. "A *very* early frost."

"Cut it out," she said. "You have a short memory. As I recall, I said I didn't want to see you again."

"We all make mistakes," he grinned, running a palm over his glossy blond hair. "Besides, I came to apologize. I didn't mean all that stuff I said about your uncle. I really like the old guy, Erika, honest."

"I'll bet you do, you and your father."

"Look, can I help it if Dad and your uncle don't get along? The best thing we can do is get together ourselves. A sort of peace treaty."

"Very touching," Erika said coldly. "And I suppose you know what your father's doing now? About the stockholder meeting?"

"I never pay any attention to that jazz."

"You know what he's trying to do, don't you? He's trying to throw Uncle Bell out on his ear. Isn't that true?"

"Business is business," Huey said reasonably. "If your uncle can't handle himself, he ought to quit. Now will you stop yammering about that lousy factory and talk about us? I want to see you this Saturday."

Erika turned her back on him, and went to the hall table. There were three envelopes on the surface, lying addressed side up.

"Well, what about it?" Huey said.

She opened the first one, and read its brief contents.

"I said what about it?" Huey said testily. "Can I see you Saturday night?"

"No," Erika smiled. "No, I'm afraid not, Huey. I've got another date."

If it hadn't been for Gabriel Lesca, Johnny would have given up his new job the second day. The Supply Department of the Lacy Company looked like the storage center for the biggest, most intricate jigsaw puzzle in the world. There must have been two thousand bins containing tools and machine parts, and if Lacy expected him to memorize them all, he was crazy.

But old Gabe Lesca gathered up the wrinkles of his lined face in an understanding grin. "It's okay, kid," he said. "Nobody expects you to catch on right away. It's taken me forty years to figure this place out. You just do what I say. I'll take the check-out tickets, and you hunt up the parts for me according to the bin numbers. Then one night a week, you can take the inventory."

"At night?"

"Yeah, Friday nights you work until eight; we can't do the inventory during working hours. Don't worry, though," he chuckled, "you get paid overtime for them extra hours."

Gabe was the oldest working man Johnny had ever seen. He would have guessed the old man was over seventy, but when he knew him well enough to ask the question, Gabe winked and said sixty-four. Johnny wasn't surprised to learn that Gabe was the company's oldest employe, that he had worked side by side with Beldon Lacy when the first Lacy Machine Shop opened at the close of World War I. When Gabe spoke of the boss, and that was often, he spoke reverently.

"They don't make 'em like Bell Lacy anymore," Gabe told him at lunch one day. "Bell built every stick and stone of this place. Yes, there's some don't like him, and maybe with good reason, but there ain't no man that don't give him credit."

"What about this Brockton?" Johnny asked. "The name seems to be a dirty word around here."

"It is," the old man said bitterly. "Around '58, when times got tough, the company was in deep water. Sales were slowing down, orders were being cancelled, and Bell was stuck with a load of new equipment that he couldn't pay for.

"Then this fella Brockton got into the act. He had something Bell needed right then. Money. He offered to buy into the place, pay for the new equipment and keep the payroll up, if Bell would give him a partnership. Well, there wasn't much else Bell could do.

"Little by little, Brockton's been trying to take over completely. He's the one talked Bell into selling shares in the company, and we got more dang owners than you can shake a stick at. That spells trouble for Bell, you wait and see."

"It's a business, isn't it?" Johnny said. "As long as Brockton's doing a good job—"

"He's out for Bell's scalp!" said the old man angrily. "And that's all he wants. That's what this dang stockholders' meeting is about. It ain't fair!" Gabe said, pounding the cafeteria table and drawing curious eyes. "It just ain't fair!"

Someone at the next table said something, and there was a round of laughter. Gabe drew himself up stiffly and finished the rest of his meal in silence.

Johnny's landlady turned out to be a motherly type. She moved the buttons on his suit jacket, and altered the cuffs of the trousers, and when he dressed for his Saturday date with Erika Lacy, he was looking a good deal more dapper.

In her note, Erika had suggested that she pick him up at the rooming house in her car. When the convertible braked at the curb, he climbed in with an embarrassed grin. "I feel like a gigolo," he said.

Erika laughed. "It's only practical that we use my car. There aren't many places you can go in Point Placid without one."

He let Erika choose the restaurant. It was a small wood-frame building almost hidden from the road. The dining room was small, the atmosphere congenial, and the menu, Johnny noted with relief, featured low-cost dishes. He ordered a bottle of red wine, and it proved to be a good investment. Talk flowed easier.

"Then you really don't mind the job?" Erika asked. "Even if you can't understand all those parts?"

"I'm learning," Johnny said cheerfully. "I can now tell you the difference between a cam and a crankpin. Also a slotter, a lapper, a honer, and a swager."

"Sounds like a foreign language."

"It is—to a guy just off a farm. If it wasn't for old Gabe, I'd really be in a fix. He's a great guy, but I'd hate to guess how old he is."

"Sixty-four," Erika smiled. "He's been one year under retirement for ages. But nobody bothers about that; they know that Gabe will quit the day he can't function at his best. The plant won't be the same without him."

She seemed saddened at the thought, or perhaps at something else. Then she looked up seriously and said:

"Johnny, could I ask you something?"

"Sure."

"When you were in the veteran's hospital, did they give you a lot of plastic surgery? For your wounds, I mean?"

He stiffened. "Yeah, sure. Why do you ask?"

"Uncle Bell said something about your insurance physical. Said you passed with flying colors."

He knew he had to be careful.

"I don't like to think about it," he said gravely. "I must have had fifty operations to patch me up."

She put her hand on his. "Don't talk about it. Just talk about the future."

"That's okay with me."

They left the restaurant at nine, and Erika asked if Johnny wanted to drive. He accepted and slid behind the wheel.

They were just turning onto the main highway when they heard the insistent beep behind them. Erika turned in the convertible seat and made an exclamation of surprise and irritation. Johnny, eyes on the mirror, watched the white sports car hugging the rear bumper and frowned.

"What goes here?"

"It's nothing," Erika said. "Just a road hog. Keep going, Johnny."

He stomped the accelerator and tried to pull away from the two-seater. The sports engine roared and moved the low-slung car within inches of the convertible's rear. When Johnny tried to shake him by making a quick turn into a side road, the white auto matched his speed and then shot out in front of him, slowing them down.

"Watch where you're going!" Johnny yelled, hitting the brake. As the white car weaved drunkenly in front of them, he cursed and brought the convertible to a halt. The driver of the sports car stopped, too.

Johnny started to slam out of the car, his eyes on fire. Erika's hand fell on his arm, restraining him.

"Don't," she said hurriedly. "It's a boy I know. He's only being funny—"

"Some joke. I think I'll teach him some manners."

"Please, Johnny!"

The driver was getting out of the bucket seat and coming toward them. He was tall and lean, with glossy blond hair, and the suit he was wearing made Johnny's twenty-dollar bargain look it.

"Hi," he said casually. "How you been, Erika?"

"Have you been following us?" she said hotly.

He grinned, and looked at Johnny. "We haven't been introduced. My name's Huey Brockton. Maybe Erika's mentioned me."

Johnny studied the handsome face for a moment. Then he said: "As a matter of fact, she did. There was a pig with an apple in its mouth in the restaurant. She said it reminded her of somebody she knew."

Huey flushed and looked at the girl.

"I wanted to see who you were dating. You didn't tell me it was the guy who swept the factory."

Johnny opened the car door, and Erika gasped.

"Please," she said. "Don't make any trouble. Huey, this is all your fault."

"Get back in your kiddy car, sonny," Johnny said.

"Who's going to make me?" When Johnny stepped up to him, he put his hand in his pocket. "Don't get wise, fella. I've got something in here that hurts."

"What is it? A rattle?"

Johnny moved. His left hand preceded him, whipping out in a jab that found Huey Brockton's chin and sent him reeling back. In the car, Erika screamed as Huey hit dirt. When he got up, his right hand was out of his pocket, the knife blade touched by moonlight.

"Don't! Don't!" Erika cried. "Leave him alone!"

Huey made a lunge in Johnny's direction. He avoided the thrust easily, sidestepping to catch Huey's arm in both hands. He slammed the arm against the side of the open convertible, the shock urging the knife out of Huey's fingers. Erika tried to reach it, but Johnny was faster. He grabbed the handle, spun Huey around in a half-nelson, and then brought the blade under his chin.

"Now," Johnny said. "Now let's see . . ."

"Leggo!" Huey grunted.

The blade edge touched his throat, and Huey's eyes bugged at the cold, deadly sensation.

"I'm going to kill you," Johnny whispered. "I'm going to slit you like a chicken."

Erika was out of the car. She pulled at Johnny's arm, but he was immovable rock. "Please, Johnny," she begged.

"I didn't want to play games with you," Johnny said. "But if I play it's for keeps. So you're going to die . . ."

Huey's eyes rolled. "Erika, help me!"

"Johnny," the girl sobbed, "Johnny, let him go!"

It took a moment, but his head began to clear. He relaxed his grip on Huey's arm, and then shoved him away. He stared down at the knife in his hand as Huey ran for his car. Then, as the sports engine roared into life, Johnny threw the knife into the woods and looked after it.

He got back into the car, dream-like. Erika took the wheel, but didn't start the car. "Johnny," she whispered.

He put his hands over his eyes.

"I was going to kill him," he said.

"You weren't. You didn't mean it."

"I was going to kill him, Erika. Like those others. Like all those others."

She shrank back against the seat.

"Others?"

He couldn't look at her.

"There were four of them. I killed them all. Don't ask me why I did it, Erika, I don't know. But I killed them all."

"I lied to you," Johnny said.

"My name isn't Brennan, it's Johnny Bree. At least, that's what they call me. I told you I'd just come off a farm job. That was half right. I was working on a farm, all right, but it wasn't the kind you know. It's a place where they grow the stuff to feed the prisoners."

"I didn't even know there was a prison near here."

"They don't call it that. They've got fancier names for it. I'm no ordinary criminal, Erika, I'm one of those mental cases you hear about. How does that make you feel?" He looked at her accusingly. "Well? When do you start screaming?"

"I won't scream, Johnny."

"Aren't you afraid? I'm a loony. Criminally insane. When I lose my head, people get killed. Like that boyfriend of yours . . ."

"But you let him go. You didn't hurt him."

"Sure," he said bitterly. "I'm making progress. That's why they trusted me to work the farm camp, because I'd been such a good boy. Those first few years—that was different. I don't remember when I arrived, or what I was doing there. It was like I was born in that place, a brand-new infant. Then—don't ask me how—I started coming out of the fog. I'd recognize a face the second time I saw it. I learned how to feed myself, dress myself, act like a rational human being. I couldn't remember much of the past, but I could get along okay in the present. But the future . . ."

"They must have been sure of the future, Johnny. They wouldn't have let you go if they weren't."

He became silent; the night sounds took over.

"But why were you there, Johnny? Do you know that?"

"That's the one thing I do know. The one thing I remember for sure. For some reason, I killed four men. It was something I couldn't help, a compulsion I couldn't control. I can't remember their names, or their faces, or where it happened. But I remember doing it, clearly."

He shut his eyes.

"One of them, I killed with a knife—just like I might have killed Huey Brockton."

Erika's gasp was involuntary. He didn't hear it.

"I strangled another one. I can still feel his throat under my fingers.

"The other two, I shot to death."

He turned to face her, and the agony of expression must have frightened her more than his confession. She moved away from him.

"I can't believe it," she said. "It must have been some sort of delusion."

"It wasn't," he said harshly. "I don't know much about myself, but I know that much. It wasn't a delusion. *It was murder.*"

He knew she was going to cry out. The scream had been suppressed too long; it emerged more of a whimper, a sound of pain rather than an expression of terror.

He got out of the car. She didn't try to stop him, and he didn't want to be stopped. He began walking down the road, in the opposite direction.

When the convertible was a speck in the distance, he heard the growl of its engine, and watched it disappear.

He was in the Point Placid bus depot an hour later, looking at a schedule that disappointed him; there would be no bus until Sunday morning at ten.

There was an empty bus in the alleyway, its doors open and its interior dark, the leather seats sweating in the high humidity. The slatted wooden benches of the waiting room were damp, too, and the atmosphere had a depressing, rancid smell.

An old man came through the doors, clanking a pail and mop together. He swirled a wave of soapy water on the tiled floor and began to swish the mop lazily in the gray foam.

"All right if I stay here?" Johnny said.

"Eh?"

"Okay if I wait in the station? I missed my bus."

The old man laughed, and went on mopping. Johnny put his feet up on the bench and lay on his back. There were eight pale yellow bulbs in the ceiling fixture, and he counted them over and over. Before long, he was asleep.

When he woke up, an early morning sun was in his face, and someone was shaking his foot.

"Come on," a voice said.

He sat up painfully, and looked at the deep-lined warrior's face of the man standing over him.

"That's a hell of a place to sleep," Beldon Lacy said. "Murder on the spine."

"Mr. Lacy—"

"Can you use a cup of coffee? There's a joint on the

corner. The coffee's hot, that's all you can say for it." He put his hand on Johnny's elbow and helped him up.

Lacy didn't say anything else until they were in the diner, with two steaming mugs in front of them. After his first sip, Lacy grunted.

"Okay," he said. "So you were running out on the job. First paycheck, and you're off. That's a heck of an attitude."

"Did Erika tell you what happened?"

"She told me."

"Then why do you think I was leaving town?"

"Look, buster. All I know is that Erika walks into the house blubbering like a kid with a busted balloon, just because you and Huey got into some kind of a tangle."

"It was more than that."

"I know; Huey pulled a knife. I always knew there was a mean streak in that twerp, it runs in the family."

"Is that all she told you?"

"No." Lacy stirred his coffee, the frown lines deepening. "She said you'd been sick. That you got into some jam when you were a kid, and got locked up for it."

Johnny's heart was thudding. Erika hadn't told her uncle the most significant fact of all. Why?

"She said you were probably going to run away," Lacy said. "I checked with your rooming house and found you weren't there, so I thought of the bus station next."

"Why?" Johnny said. "Why'd you bother?"

"How do I know?" Lacy growled. "Because Erika wanted me to, I guess. And besides, you can't run out on old Gabe. He was just getting used to you. So I'll expect you back on the job tomorrow."

"I can't do that," Johnny said.

Lacy's hand went to his shoulder. It wasn't just a friendly gesture.

"I'm not asking you. I'm telling you. Nobody runs out on me, buddy, me *or* my niece. Nobody has to know anything about your past, and I'll see that our friend Huey keeps his mouth shut. Not that he'll want to brag about what happened."

Johnny finished the last inch of coffee in his mug.

"All right," he said. "You're the boss."

On Wednesday, Johnny put a new check-out system into

operation. It was his own idea, involving a day-to-day ticketing of parts that would make Friday's inventory sessions a great deal faster. Gabe Lesca had seen the common sense of the plan as soon as Johnny described it.

"You watch it, boy," he warned good-naturedly. "They'll yank you off this cushy job and turn you into an executive."

Johnny had blushed and looked pleased.

Friday night, Johnny left the plant at the last shrill of the five-o'clock whistle, leaving Gabe in the locker room. He wasn't due back until six for the final inventory of the week, and he spent the intervening hour at the diner across the road. The food was greasy, but he didn't notice.

When he returned to the plant, he went to the supply room and started going over the check-out slips. He wasn't going to benefit from the results of the new inventory system for another week, so he had a good two hours of work ahead of him. Then he had a sudden concern. Would there be another week? Or would the stockholder's meeting that was scheduled for Monday put an end to his new life?

Howard Brockton. He said the name aloud and realized he had never seen the man who was causing so much grief in the Lacy Company and Lacy household.

He bent to his work. He didn't look up again until eight-fifteen.

On his way out of the plant, he took the short cut through the administration building to reach the main gate.

At the end of a long corridor of executive offices, there was a partly opened door, spilling yellow light onto the polished floor. Somebody was working late in administration, too.

As he came closer, he saw Howard Brockton's name on the wall plaque. If he went by slow enough, he might actually glimpse the ogre in his lair.

What he saw startled him. The man was behind a large oak desk in the office, but his head was resting on the blotter. The light of the desk lamp gleamed on a bald scalp, and put a highlight in the circular stain that spread out from his chin.

He walked into the office, and said:

"Mr. Brockton?"

He touched the man's shoulder. Then he saw the color of the stain, and knew he was beyond response. He pushed him back in the chair, and saw that he had walked in on a dead man. The left half of his skull had been crushed, the skin of his cheek split like a ripe melon, the blood still wet on his face. He was a small-featured man, with colorless eyes. If there was cruelty and calculation in him, it must have registered in his expression, and all that was wiped away by death.

Then Johnny heard the rattling, heavy-footed sound of the Lacy night watchman, coming down the hall, and he grasped the real horror of the moment.

If he were found in this office, how could he explain it? How could he answer the questions they were bound to ask? Who was he? Where did he come from? What was his real name? Why was he hired? And then his answers. *I'm Johnny Bree. I'm a murderer. I've escaped from an asylum for the criminally insane. And I'm innocent, innocent!*

The watchman's footsteps halted outside the door. His hand was on the knob, and he was pulling it the wrong way. Open.

"Mr. Brockton?"

Johnny made his bolt for freedom. It meant a headlong rush at the guard, and surprise was his best weapon. But the man's reflexes were good; he flailed out and caught Johnny's arm. Johnny lashed out with his right fist and broke away, running down the hall even after the shouted warning.

"Stop! Stop or I'll have to shoot!"

At the end of the corridor, his soles slid on the polished floor for the last six inches, and he tugged at the knob of the outside door. Then he was in the courtyard, past the unguarded gate before the watchman could hinder him. But even as he went on a dead run into town, he knew the worst of the night was still to come, when the watchman found what had been left behind in Howard Brockton's office.

He climbed into a taxi and gave the Lacys' address, without knowing whether he wanted to see Erika or his boss. Then he discovered that it was a radio cab; that meant its low-powered network was available for com-

mandeering by the police. If they were after him already
the bored, nasal commands of the dispatcher might be in-
terrupted at any moment. *To all drivers . . . be on the
lookout for . . .*

But no message came; they climbed the slope of Sycamore
Hills, and he was safely at the Lacy front door.

Erika answered his ring. She was wearing a black dress
with some of the buttons undone.

"Johnny . . ."

"I've got to talk to you, Erika. Will you let me in?"

He gave her no time to think about it. He stepped inside
and closed the door quickly.

"Is your uncle home?"

"No. He's at his club. What's wrong, Johnny?"

"I've got something to tell you. I wanted to tell you
uncle, too. It's about Brockton."

"Howard Brockton?"

"He's dead, Erika. He was killed."

She put a closed fist to her mouth.

"Don't think that!" Johnny yelled. "I was working late
at the plant; I found his body. But the night watchman
caught me in the office and I ran away. He saw me, Erika
they'll think I had something to do with it!"

She was staring ahead, unresponsive. He grabbed her
thin shoulders and shook them.

"Believe me!" he shouted. "Believe me, Erika, please!"

The phone was ringing in the living room. Erika moved
towards the doorway, waiting to see if he would stop her
He didn't, but only followed and watched.

"Yes, Uncle Bell . . ."

He took the phone from her ear.

". . . on his way there," he heard Bell Lacy say. "That's
what the cab dispatcher told us. So get in the car and beat
it, go to the Club and stay there until I arrive. Got that?"

Johnny pointed to the mouthpiece and nodded.

"Yes," Erika said. "Yes, I understand, Uncle Bell."

"I should have known better," the voice said. "I never
should have let him into the plant. Now look at the mess.

"Uncle Bell, listen—"

Johnny clutched her arm, warning her with pain.

"All right," she said. "I'll leave right now. But I can
believe Johnny did it. It's just not possible."

"He did it, all right, he was caught in the act. You told

me yourself he was a killer; maybe he thought he was doing me some kind of favor, the poor slob. Don't waste time, Erika!"

She hung up. "What are you going to do?" she whispered.

"Get me your car keys!"

She went to the hall closet. He came after her and saw her struggling with a coat on a hanger. He pushed her aside and reached down to the closet floor.

There was a double-barreled shotgun leaning against the side. He picked it up, glowering at her.

"No, Johnny," she said. "I swear I wasn't going to do that. I was looking for the keys."

"Get them."

She found them in the pocket of a raincoat and handed them over. He took them and went to the door, but as he opened it, the light burst against him like an exploding shell. He slammed it shut and leaned against it.

"What is it?" Erika said. "What's happening?"

"The police. They're out there already."

He hoisted the shotgun and motioned her back to the living room. There was a drumbeat in his body, pacing his actions. He went to the front window and pulled back the curtain; there was a black-and-white trooper's car out front, its spotlight trained on the doorway. A figure moved into its glare, and raised a bell-shaped object to his lips.

"Brennan!" the amplified voice said. "Brennan, this is Captain Demerest of the State Police. This is not an arrest. We want you to come out of there so we can talk to you."

Erika moaned. "Do what they say, Johnny!"

"We can't wait too long, Brennan," the voice said. "Every minute you stay in there counts against you."

A second car was pulling up the hill, its brakes screeching. Four troopers piled out, their arms laden with weapons. Johnny snorted, and edged up to the window.

"I'm not coming out!" he yelled.

"Send the girl out, Brennan! Don't make things worse!"

He turned to Erika, his face agonized.

"I can't," he said. "I just can't do that, Erika." Then, to the police: "Don't try and break in! I've got a gun in here! I'll kill her if you try to break in!"

He moved away from the window and went to her.

"I won't hurt you," he said. "You know I won't, Erika."

"This can't help you, Johnny. You'll have to give in to them, sooner or later."

"Later, then. Later!"

It was later, much later, before he heard another stir from the cordon outside the stone house. For more than an hour, the law forces of town and state were conferring on appropriate steps. For Johnny, sitting in the living room with the shotgun across his legs, the postponement was a respite; it was torment.

Then the portable loudspeaker sounded again.

"Johnny! Can you hear me? This is Beldon Lacy!"

Erika whimpered at the familiar voice.

"Listen to me, Johnny. Nobody wants to hurt you. Throw that gun away and come out here."

"Please," Erika murmured. "Listen to him, Johnny. You know Uncle Bell likes you . . ."

"You think I didn't hear what he said on the phone? He said I was a killer . . ." The word jarred him as he said it. "How did he know that, Erika? He said you'd told him I'd been sick. But nothing about those . . . men I killed."

"I told him," Erika said. "Of course, I told him, Johnny, I always tell him everything."

"Then he knew I was a murderer. But he still wanted me to work for him? Why, Erika?"

"Johnny!" the loudspeaker boomed. "Will you listen to reason. You've got friends out here. We want to help—"

"Why?" Johnny said harshly. "Why should he want a killer on the payroll? I'll tell you why, Erika. So he could have a fall guy . . ."

He rushed to the window.

"Send Bell Lacy in here!" he bellowed. "I'll talk to Bell Lacy and nobody else!"

"Uncle Bell! Uncle Bell, don't—"

He shoved Erika away, with enough violence to send her careening against the sofa. She began to cry, the first tears since his arrival.

Then a figure separated itself from the crowd.

"Don't hurt him," Erika sobbed. "Don't hurt him, Johnny."

The knock on the front door was bold. Johnny went to

the hall and trained the muzzle of the shotgun in its direction. The door opened, and Lacy was there.

"Where's Erika?"

She ran to him, and he put his arm around her.

"Get away from her," Johnny said.

"Put the gun down, Johnny, you won't need it anymore. We know how Howard Brockton was killed."

Johnny laughed. "Sure you do. And so do I. Because you planned the whole thing. You knew I was a killer, and that's why you wanted me around the plant."

"That's not true, Johnny."

"Erika told you about those four men I killed. Only you wouldn't admit it. You made me think you didn't know."

"All right, so I knew. But Erika said you were cured; they wouldn't have released you if you weren't."

"You're a liar! You wanted an alibi, that's all you wanted! And I was elected."

He raised the shotgun.

"Brennan!" the loudspeaker boomed outside. "Brennan, there's somebody here to see you! Can you hear me, Brennan?"

Johnny moved cautiously to the window, and pulled aside the curtain. Another car had arrived on the scene, a gray civilian car without markings. There were two men climbing out of the front seat.

"Listen to me, Brennan. These men want to speak to you. They've come to help you."

Johnny shielded his eyes against the glare and tried to make out the newcomers. One was a short round man wearing a crumpled business suit. The other was tall and angular and wore the olive-green uniform of a Marine Corps officer.

"Colonel Joe," Johnny whispered.

"What is it?" Erika said. "Who are they?"

"Colonel Joe!" Johnny shouted, his eyes widening.

He looked wildly between the girl and her uncle, and then broke for the hallway, clutching the shotgun in one hand. He flung open the door and ran out, his face strangely exalted, his eyes glowing in the lights of the police vehicles. The shot that came from the nervous ring of officers dropped him before he was three yards from the house, and he pitched forward into the gravel of the driveway and lay still.

When Erika walked into the hospital room, the Marine officer was at Johnny's bedside, and for the first time, she saw the caduceus insignia on his lapel. His hair was gray, but except for the wisdom in his eyes, he was still a young man.

"You must be Erika," he smiled. "I'm Joe Gillem."

She looked at Johnny, who grinned weakly.

"Sorry," he said. "I've been doing a lot of talking. A lot of it's been about you."

"How do you feel?"

"Right at home. They got the bullet out of my hip, and I'll probably limp around a while, but I'm okay."

"It's better than that," the Colonel said. "Much better. Johnny's starting to remember."

Erika held her breath. "Remember?"

"The past. The truth about himself. Somehow, his escape accomplished more than his whole confinement. Not that we recommend it as therapy, but it worked in this case."

"Escape?" Erika said.

"It's true," Johnny said. "That's one thing I was too afraid to tell you, Erika. I wasn't let out; I ran away."

She looked at the Colonel, her question unspoken.

"No," he smiled. "I don't think he'll have to go back, Miss Lacy, not now. He'll be what we call an out-patient."

"Patient?"

"Did you think he was a prisoner? No, Miss Lacy, it wasn't a jail. It's a psychiatric hospital for veterans. Johnny was there because he had lost all conscious memory of his year in Korea; all he had left was guilt. . . .

"It happened in the fall of '53, on Heartbreak Ridge. Johnny was on patrol, and after his sergeant was killed by snipers, he took command. They were behind Communist lines; that was the kind of war we were fighting. Suddenly, they found themselves facing an artillery barrage, and, in trying to get away, they got caught in a pocket in plain sight of a machine-gun nest. The only hope of getting out alive was to put it out of action. That's what Johnny did; under covering fire, he got behind the nest and threw a grenade. The gun was out of action, all right, but four of the enemy were still alive.

"It was the first time he had to kill face to face. He was eighteen years old. He shot two of them and was forced to bayonet another. He lost his M-1 that way, and the last man had to be garroted. Those were his four 'victims,' Miss Lacy, the 'murders' he's been guilty of.

"He was brought back to a field hospital in a state of shock, no wounds. He was in a catatonic state and didn't snap out of it for months. His memory was gone; all he could recall was the fact that he was a murderer . . .

"When we heard the television broadcast about Howard Brockton's murder and saw the plant photo of Johnny, I knew who it was—and that the police were after the wrong man. That's when I came over, with Dr. Winterhaus, the chief psychiatrist. We've both been spending a lot of time with Johnny, and we're convinced he's coming back to health."

Erika had been listening with wonder and mounting happiness, but when she turned to Johnny, she found his expression melancholy.

"I'm so glad for you, Johnny . . ."

"Yeah," he said. "But you know what it means, don't you? It means I must have been right about your uncle . . ."

She looked swiftly at the Colonel.

"Then he doesn't know? Nobody's told him?"

"Know what?" Johnny said.

Erika went to the bedside, and took his hand.

"It wasn't Uncle Bell, Johnny. It was poor old Gabe who killed Brockton, poor unhappy Gabe . . ."

"Gabe?"

"Yes," Erika said sadly. "He thought he was helping Uncle Bell; he went to Brockton's office and argued with him; the argument ended with old Gabe hitting him with some tool he carried. He never even realized how seriously he had hurt him; then he learned, and came to Uncle Bell to tell him the truth."

"Poor Gabe," Johnny said mournfully. "What will they do to him, Erika?"

"Uncle Bell swears he'll fight for him. You can say what you like about Uncle Bell, but loyalty is like a religion to him . . ."

"Where is he now? Your uncle?"

"He said he'd be here at four o'clock. He wants to talk to you about something; I think it's that new inventory system of yours." She held his hand tighter. "If he offers you a job, Johnny, something in the front office, would you take it? Or would you be stubborn about it?"

"I don't know. He's not obliged to me for anything."

"But would you take it?"

"I'd have to think about it."

"I knew it," Erika said peevishly. "You're going to be stubborn. I could have predicted that. What do *you* do in a case like that, Doctor?"

Colonel Joe grinned. "I dunno. Guess I'd try some friendly persuasion."

She tried it and it worked.

POINT THE MAN OUT!

Duane Decker

Judy picked the last of the clean laundry off the line and dropped the pieces into the wicker clothesbasket at her feet. Her shorts were a bright yellow, her long legs, tanned. She appeared an idealized picture of a suburban housewife.

As Judy reached for the basket, she faced the Post Road, which ran past the house. It was at that moment that she noticed the parked gray sedan, saw the man at the wheel staring at her.

She turned abruptly, picked up the almost-filled basket and walked quickly toward the kitchen door, feeling a creeping sense of disquiet at the intensity of the man's stare. Whoever he was he had a lot of nerve. The wrong kind.

The neat little white house with its dark green blinds had been built by Brad right after their marriage, in an undeveloped section well outside the city. They had both liked the feeling of living away from noise and soot, surrounded by trees instead of being hemmed in by neighbors. And the property had been cheap. As Brad had said, it would increase in value when the city grew toward them. Later, they could sell for a nice profit and build a bigger place farther out. So far, though, real-estate development out their way had been slow. Only two other houses had been built, and they were distant.

Once safely inside the kitchen, Judy set the basket on the floor and started to pick out the towels and things that didn't need to be ironed. Suddenly, she thought she heard the front door open. That startled her.

She glanced at her wristwatch. No, Brad wouldn't be home yet. It was not even five, and he seldom arrived before five-thirty. She felt a ripple of uneasiness as she dropped the towels back into the basket and hurried into the living room.

The man from the car stood there. He had a sort of twisted grin on his face. It was not a natural or happy grin. Glassy.

He was young, around twenty-five. He was of average height and build, neither handsome nor homely. He was no one you would be apt to notice when you passed him on the street. If you remembered him at all, it would be because of what he wore: navy-blue sports jacket, with gleaming white buttons, and dark gray slacks. His eyes were close-set and his breath smelled strongly of whisky. Instinctively, Judy drew back.

"Well," he said, "I always knew I'd catch up with you sometime, Babes."

She stared at him. Was he insane? "Who *are* you?" she demanded. There was something about him that was as unreal and terrifying as a bad dream.

"Ho ho! You don't remember me, honey, is that it?"

"I never saw you before in my life," Judy said.

"Well, I saw you," he said. "In the courtroom, when you pointed me out. And then—your picture in the papers."

"I never *had* my picture in the papers."

"Modest, you're real modest. I suppose now you can con me that you never lived in New York?"

"Certainly I lived there, once," Judy said. "Everybody has at some time or other. I want to know why you're here." She was trying to sound braver than she felt. She backed up as he advanced.

He removed a pack of cigarettes and matches from his jacket pocket. "It's a downright miracle," he said. "You know, I never really thought it would happen. Wasn't much chance. Anyhow, ever since I got out of that place up in old Ossining, I've roamed. I have roamed and I have looked. At women's faces. All kinds. Some of them pretty young faces, too. Like the one in the courtroom, in the newspapers. *Your* face, Floss."

Judy kept on backing up. The man was most certainly mad. She edged closer and closer to the telephone. He didn't seem to notice. She wanted to keep him talking until she could get close enough to grab the phone, grab it and dial the operator and scream for help.

"Why did you look for my face?" she asked.

"You know why, Lolita," he said. "Because you were the one who pointed me out."

"Pointed you out? To whom? Why?"

She was almost against the telephone table now. He was so absorbed by their conversation that he did not even pause to light his cigarette.

"Shall I refresh your memory, Peachy?" he asked. "You were walking into the delicatessen on Third Avenue that night. A man rushed past you. You looked at him as he came out. Then went on inside. You found the guy who ran the place unconscious, pistol-whipped, the cash register rifled. You called the police. You described the man. The police picked up a dozen men, me included, and we all looked sort of alike. Because there is nothing unusual about the way I look, is there?"

"No," Judy said. "I noticed that when I first saw you. Five minutes ago."

He laughed, more of a snort than a laugh. "Five minutes ago? Five years ago, you mean. That's when they told you to point the man out. And you pointed me out of the line-up. I didn't do it, you hear? But because of you I was stuck in Sing-Sing for four years. Because of you I lost my wife and my kid—my boy. And I never did it, you hear? *I never did it!*"

She was smack up against the telephone table now. Her hands behind her touched the phone.

She made one final effort to communicate with him. She said in a quiet voice, "You're making the same mistake you accuse me of having made. I didn't point you out. It must have been somebody else who looked a lot like me."

"It was you," he said.

"You've been drinking," she said. "You're mixed up about it. You have to be because I wasn't there."

He shook his head. "I studied your face in that court-room, and I studied your picture in the paper. I still have that picture. You want to see it, sweetheart? It's right here in my wallet."

By this time, she was sure he was beyond reason. And she asked herself what chance she'd have with him after she grabbed the phone and screamed police. Finally, he was about to light the cigarette. He had it in his mouth, when suddenly the back door slammed. It slammed shut, with what sounded like a frenzy of energy behind it. The man spat the unlighted cigarette out of his mouth and strode over toward her. But he paused, midway, as quick feet tapped across the kitchen floor.

"Mother?" called a young, thin voice.

And then Toby walked through the doorway.

Toby was nine. He had red hair like Brad's, and freckles, and his father's purposeful look. He took in the scene, his eyes wide with alarm.

"*Run*, Toby!" Judy cried. "Get help! Run!"

The man grabbed her, tried to pin her arms to her sides. But she managed to twist free. The man caught her in two quick steps. He spun her around. She screamed and kicked at his ankles.

He struck her then. And as she sank to the floor, she saw Toby rush at the man, his small arms striking out even before he reached him.

"You fixed my boy," the man shouted at her, "so I'll fix yours!"

Then she saw the man hit Toby, and kick at him when he was on the floor. And then he was looking down at her, saying, "Now we're all even, Babes. Next time you point the man out, be sure."

There was the sound of the front door shutting; so she knew he was gone. And, as she crawled to the telephone, she was aware that Toby was utterly still. She picked up the phone and said, "Get me a hospital—emergency. . . ."

It was dusk when Brad Durant turned the car into the driveway. The absence of lights inside the house didn't disturb him. He remembered that when he'd left for the office in the morning, Judy had mentioned the possibility of Grace Nichols picking her up in the afternoon for a shopping tour in town. No doubt it had worked out; and they'd probably stopped at the Nichols' en route home, for cocktails. He'd been out of town all afternoon; so if Judy had tried to reach him at the office to join her at the Nichols', she had drawn a blank.

It wasn't until he unlocked the front door, stepped inside and snapped on the hall light that he became aware that something *was* wrong. There was disorder in the living room: chairs pushed out of their usual places, a scatter rug askew, a broken cigarette and a match packet on the floor. And—where was Toby, come to think of it? Not at the Nichols' cocktail party.

He rushed to the telephone stand, which was not set in its usual corner. There he saw the envelope jutting out from under the phone. Before he read it, he recognized Judy's rounded handwriting. It said:

"Brad—Toby and I are at the Memorial Hospital. An accident. Will explain when you arrive. Don't worry." And it was signed, "Judy."

Don't worry.

He turned and shot out of the front door.

It was a private room, all nice and white and antiseptic, and Judy's mouth was puffed and purplish, the lips split. A kind of horror too great for him to contain seized him as he looked down at her.

He knelt by the side of the bed. In a thick voice he said, "Judy! Darling! Can you hear me, Judy? They said they shot you full of stuff, but, Judy, can you tell me what happened?"

She did not answer, and he gently stroked her forehead. Then words, incoherent at first, came from her lips.

"He . . . he thought I was somebody else . . . a delicatessen on Third Avenue . . . out of his mind . . . white buttons . . ."

It made no sense to him, of course. He kissed her forehead tenderly. "Try to tell me, Judy, I must know. I've *got* to know what happened. And—about Toby."

She swallowed. She nodded. "I—I'll try, Brad. The police were here . . . I couldn't make sense. I'll try."

Slowly, tortuously, she managed to give him a picture of the revolting thing that had happened because of the mistaken identity in the madman's mind. She told him of the quick arrival of the ambulance. The doctor, who had just left her, said she suffered mainly from shock. But Toby— her voice broke. Finally, she could tell him about Toby.

"The doctor said poor Toby's right eye had been seriously damaged by all those punches. It's so awful. And when he was kicked. That man kicked him in the head. The doctor said Toby *might* see out of that eye again, but not to expect too much. His hearing—" Her voice collapsed again.

"His hearing?" Brad said.

"He—he might hear again with the ear that was injured. But probably not."

"What did the police have to say?"

She shook her head. "The sedatives I had. I—I just couldn't make sense. They said they'd come back when I could talk."

"The man," Brad said. "What did he look like?"

"He—he's sort of ordinary," she said. "He isn't tall or short, thin or fat. Kind of hard to describe . . ."

Listening, fists and teeth tightly clenched, Brad knew he had to hunt the man down and kill him. Himself. He had a head start on the police. They hadn't found out a thing yet. But they would, soon.

Nothing else would do except for him to find the man by himself. Nothing else would settle it, in his mind. Toby, handicapped for life; Judy, with her beautiful face marred. The slow, devious machinery of the law could never satisfy him.

Why, if the police caught up with the man, some slick lawyer would get him off with a year, or maybe just a few months. While Toby would suffer through his entire life. And Judy . . . He had never known feelings so immediate and savage and final. The mere thought of the man remaining alive was more than he could bear.

"Judy," he said, controlling his voice, "how long do you figure the man has been on his way?"

"What time is it now, Brad?"

"Twenty past six."

"It was a little before five when—when he got to our house."

So, Brad figured, the man had roughly an hour and a half start. He was thinking with the speed of anger. The man had to be somebody just passing through. He'd made that clear—that he "roamed." He might be a traveling salesman, an itinerant worker, or—

"Describe him for me again, Judy."

She described the man again. But it didn't help. The man sounded so terribly nondescript, so much like a hundred others you see on the street every day in the week.

Then Brad remembered something.

"Judy," he said, "before you started to make sense, you said something about 'white buttons.' "

"Oh! Brad yes, yes! You'd notice his clothes!"

"If he hasn't already put on something else," Brad said bitterly. "What were they like?"

"It almost seemed," she said, "as though they were *meant* to be remembered. A navy-blue sports jacket with very *bright* white buttons. And gray slacks."

It sounded sort of nautical to Brad. It wasn't the kind of jacket you ordinarily saw around town.

Something that had stuck in his mind, something he was feeling for, suddenly came to the surface. He said, "Judy—when I walked into the house, the place was all messed up. Things had been pushed around. I saw a cigarette and a book of matches on the floor. Were those—*his?*"

Her eyes opened wide now. "Brad—yes, yes they were! I remember. He was about to light a cigarette when Toby came in. He spit the cigarette out. Probably, he dropped the matches."

Now he had something. "Have the police been out to the house?" he asked her.

"They—they're waiting to talk to me."

He arose. "I'll tell them you can talk now," he said. "I'll be back after awhile, Judy." He leaned over the bed, carefully touched his lips to her bruised ones.

"Brad, what are you going to do?"

"Tell the police you can talk to them now. Then, honey, I'm going home and going to sleep."

He was aware that she was staring after him as he left the hospital room.

When he reached the house, he went immediately to where he remembered seeing the match packet. And sure enough, there it was on the floor in front of the telephone stand. There was an unlit cigarette, somewhat crumpled, near it. He picked up the match packet.

"Pink Cloud Motel—Route 24."

That wrapped it up. He was way ahead of the police. He even knew the place, knew exactly where it was. Not more than a twenty-minute drive. To hell with the police and with the defense lawyers who were trained to obstruct justice.

He went out to the garage, where he kept his fishing equipment. Inside a green-metal tackle box, he found his long-bladed hunting knife nested in its leather sheath. He put it in his inside jacket pocket.

It was dark when he reached the Pink Cloud Motel, a fancy place with swimming pool and cocktail lounge. There were a few cars in the parking lot at the side of the lounge. He looked them over, slowly, one by one. There was a gray sedan.

He parked in front of the motel. Then he got out of the car and stepped to a window near the entrance. He peered inside.

The bar was a long rectangle with subdued lighting. He could not make out the faces at the far end, it was that dim, but the customers near the front were clearly defined. And his heart tripped fast when he spotted the man nearest the window, who was talking with a blonde.

The man wore a navy-blue jacket with gleaming white buttons, and he was wearing gray slacks. Everything else about him fitted Judy's descpription, too—average height, average build, average everything.

Brad waited by the window. Ten minutes went by. Fifteen. Twenty. Finally, he saw the blonde pat the man on the shoulder and move off. The man finished his drink in a gulp, left some change spread on the bar and turned toward the front door, walking hurriedly.

Brad slipped around the corner of the building, to the parking lot. He removed the long-bladed hunting knife from its sheath. He stood perfectly still in the dark shadows of the motel as the sound of the footsteps came closer.

The man in the navy-blue jacket, with gleaming white buttons, walked around the corner. He did not see Brad. Brad waited, to be sure. If the man went to the gray sedan . . .

The man went to the gray sedan. Brad reached him as he started to open the door. The man heard him and turned. Something in Brad's face must have filled him with sudden panic. Then the man saw the knife in Brad's hand and he tried to run.

Brad blocked his path. When he tried to dodge around him, Brad tripped him up. The man landed on his stomach, rolled over onto his back.

Brad stood over him. The man was helpless now. Brad spoke only ten words before he plunged the knife: "You called on my wife and son two hours ago—"

He returned to the car, the knife back inside its sheath, inside his coat pocket. He turned on the ignition and buzzed the motor. And then, just as he started to make the turn onto the highway, the door of the cocktail lounge opened. He hit the brakes and stared.

The man who walked out wore a navy-blue jacket with gleaming white buttons, and gray slacks. He was average height. Average build. He stood there looking uncertainly around him.

The door opened again. This time a second man emerged, and a third and a fourth—and they all wore navy-blue jackets with gleaming white buttons and gray slacks. They were all of average height and build. These four must have been at the dim end of the bar.

Brad heard one of them call: "Fred! Hey, Fred, where the hell are you?"

A second one of the group walked over to the door of Brad's car and peered inside. He said, "Dads, did you see a real cool cat dressed like us come out of here a couple minutes ago?"

"I just got here," Brad said. He could hear the sound of his own breathing. "Why—why are all of you dressed exactly the same?"

The young man grinned. "You mean to say, Ace, you never heard of the Five Blue Notes? We play the progressive stuff. We don't mess with the Dixie."

"You—you're a band?"

"Best five-piece combo in the land, Jack. Well, got to find old Freddie-cat. He's our trombone man. Can't hit the road without old Fred. Maybe he went to our car out back. Well, got to go, Champ. We shouldda cut out like hours ago, Clyde."

Brad watched him join the other three. They headed toward the gray sedan.

He gunned the motor and swung the car onto the highway. He couldn't kill four more times, just to make sure he'd killed the right man. He didn't see how he could go to the police about what he'd just done. Not now. Because the odds that he'd killed the right man were overwhelmingly against him.

CROOKS, SATCHELS, AND SELMA

Michael Brett

I'm sitting in my room minding my own business, which ain't very hard, because right now I'm kind of like unemployed. But like my educated friend, Hot Rod Washburne says, "This ain't the worst thing in the world because there's people out of work all the time." Hot Rod says that sometimes big executives drawing down twenty and twenty-five gees are sometimes out of work for five–six months before they find a position. So why should I worry? Sooner or later something's got to turn up. Anyway, that's what Hot Rod says and I listen when he says something, because he's a pretty smart guy. He's thirty-eight years old and I ain't never seen him work a day in his life.

And that ain't easy, no matter what anybody tells you. You can beat working if you're born with a silver spoon, but from what I hear, more people are born without spoons than with them. I think Lincoln said something about that, too.

So why worry, I keep telling myself. All it gets you is a lot of gray hairs and I don't need that. I'm a good-looking guy, young, very smart and also a clean-cut type. So in a way it doesn't make sense that I'm not working. Maybe the real reason is because I don't have an honorable discharge from the Navy. It's not exactly a dishonorable discharge. It's one of those new secret classifications, which says that the United States Navy and me haven't parted company on the best of terms.

Like they say, there's a girl at the root of my troubles, and in my case it's Selma Litts, who's a Wave. I remember it like it happened yesterday.

I first met Selma when we were stationed in Florida. I took one look at this big blonde chick and I knew that we were made for each other.

She feels the same way, because when I kiss her she trembles and that's a sure sign that she's crazy for me. We're two splendid specimens. I'm handsome and smart and she's gorgeous, fills her uniform nicely, and we have this large animal magnetism going for us.

I got it bad, and I find that after two dates she's shaking and trembling even worse than before. I find it very rough to stay in my barracks at night when she's over in the Waves' barracks, so I sneak out one night and I get by the Marine sentry stationed outside of her place. I meet her in the washroom at three o'clock in the morning and we start hugging and kissing. An hour later I sneak back to my barracks like a common criminal, but it was worth it. She was trembling so good she had me trembling right with her.

But when I get back to my barracks, I've got trouble. It's my luck that the chief petty officer decides to pull a bed check. Naturally he doesn't find me sacked out, because I'm not there. I get ten hours' extra duty for that, but what with Selma's trembling and all that, I figure it's worth it.

I'm back over to the Waves' barracks the next night and things are getting real rough for Selma and me. She's shaking and I'm shaking and things can't go on like that. I already know that I love her, so I ask her to marry me.

You've got to see Selma to understand. All a guy has to do is take one look and he falls in love with Selma Litts right away. Well, I figure with all the trembling and quivering that she's going to grab my offer.

She puts her hands on my shoulders and says, "Harold, how long have you been in the Navy?"

"Almost six years," I answer quickly, because I've got a good sense of time.

"Harold, you're still a seaman. How can I marry a man I outrank?"

"But those things happen," I explain. "I was a first-class aviation machinist . . ."

"Never mind what you were. I heard about how you were running a still on Johnston Island, and how you were broken down to seaman first. The whole base knows about your record. Before I marry a man, he's got to be as solid as a rock. I want a house and kids, and money to start marriage with."

"How much do you want?" I ask. "Ten thousand be enough for you? I can start up a little operation right here on the base and I'll have that for you in no time."

"There you go again, trying for shortcuts. In the first place, I want more than ten thousand. It used to be ten thousand, but prices are up, real estate is sky high. It'll have to be fifteen thousand dollars. My hitch will be up soon, and if we have fifteen thousand we can get married."

So that was how things stood then in the Waves' washroom, with me holding her, and her shaking and telling me, "Stop, Harold. You don't have any right."

That's what she thought. I was going to marry her, and I figured that gave me certain rights.

Anyway, I hear somebody coming into the barracks and, when I stick my head out of the washroom, I see two Wave officers. And just about then I learn how sneaky the Navy really is. Sending Wave officers around to pull a bed check on the enlisted Waves! That's about as underhanded as anybody can get. I can understand the Navy checking on the guys. But the Waves? That's going too far. It's an invasion of privacy, is what it is.

I'm no fool though. I already told you that I was smart. The minute I see them, I make a mad dash to one of the empty bunks, jump in and pull the blanket over my head.

Selma stays right where she is, in the washroom. Why not? She's got a perfect right to be there.

But talk about those Navy Wave officers. Not only did they pull a bed check, but they count Selma too. That's like hitting below the belt. There are supposed to be twenty-four sleeping Waves in the barracks. They get twenty-five as a final figure, and in a Wave barracks having one more is worse than having one less.

Right away one of those officers starts blowing her whistle. It sounded like Battle Stations, Hit the Deck, the Enemy is in Sight, and all that kind of stuff.

Waves start rolling out of their sacks and snapping to attention, but I stayed under the blanket like I was frozen, until one of the officers pulls the blanket off me. I didn't even bother to salute, but was off and running like I was in the second at Hialeah and I had a fast start.

I heard lots of screaming in back of me and somebody was yelling, "Halt! Halt!"

But I paid no attention. The way it figured was that I'd run right over the parade grounds to my barracks, but I'd be traveling so fast nobody would be able to see me. All they'd see would be a shadowy form whizzing through the dark.

I flew through the door and there's the Marine sentry. He ain't big, but he's carrying a World War Two Garand pointing right at my belt. When he said, "Halt!" he was thirty-two feet, five inches tall. And I halted. Make no mistake about that.

I hit the brakes and skidded right up to him. I laughed and put my hands over my head and said, "Kamarad! Give me a break, will ya, buddy?"

I never did get to find out if he would, because just then the Wave officers come running out and also some of the girls in their nighties. The Marine sees all these kids running around in their underwear and it musta upset him, because he pulls the trigger and a slug zips by my right ear and buries itself in the barracks.

Right away there's real excitement. Three Waves faint. Searchlights start going on all over the base. It always happens when there's any kind of trouble at the Waves' barracks. In fact, I think the Admiral has got a direct wire to any trouble over there. Usually, if there's any trouble at the enlisted men's barracks, the O.D. handles it. He drives out in his Jeep with a couple other guys, like civilized human beings, but that doesn't apply when there's trouble at the Waves' barracks. All of a sudden six Jeeps come careening up and there's brass all over the place.

I don't need anyone to tell me that I've got big trouble. There's a court martial and it takes five pages just to read off all the charges. They say I was A.W.O.L., discovered in the Waves' barracks, out of bounds, and I fled the scene of the crime, whatever it is. I get myself a Marine lawyer, and he tells me that the brass is willing to make a deal.

All I have to do is give them the name of the Wave I was visiting and they'll lessen the charges. It seems that in all the excitement, while all the screaming and yelling and fainting was going on, Selma Litts slipped back into her bed, and what with all the confusion and everything, nobody was able to remember which bed I was in.

Well, you know I wouldn't spill the beans about any

woman, let alone the one I was going to marry. I'm a gentleman, always was, and besides, I'm kind of suspicious as to why everybody wants to know who she is.

I do a couple of months in the brig, and when I get out, Selma tells me she thinks that I was very gallant for not revealing her name, but just the same what she said before still goes. She wants money in the bank even more now, since I'm an ex-Navy con. The Navy gives me my walking papers right after that and I go out to face the world.

With my brain power, it figures there'll be many companies looking to hire me immediately. I read in the newspapers how research engineers who can offer creativity are in great demand, so it comes as a surprise when the companies turn my applications down, just because I ain't a research analyst or an engineer. What these companies ignore is the fact that I've got imagination and creativity.

Anyway, now I'm thinking about all that's happened to me, and I'm just sitting looking out of my window, taking in the view that comes with my cheap room. It's hardly what you call magnificent. I'm on the second floor facing a gritty brick wall, and the rear door of the National Chemical Farmers Bank, which is always locked. The bank doesn't use it because that door faces out into the dirty alley.

There's a bunch of rubble down there, rusted tin cans, some old shoes, newspapers and lots of litter, and two alley cats hissing at each other. It's a gray day for me. I don't have a job, I don't have fifteen thousand dollars so I can marry Selma Litts, and looking at all the garbage in the alley makes me feel even lower.

All of a sudden the back door of the bank opens and two guys carrying guns come running out. One of them is wearing a lumber jacket and he's got a head like a chunk of poured cement. Then all hell breaks loose. The bank alarm goes off and two other guys carrying satchels come running out of the bank. It don't take more than a second and a bank guard is out in the alley firing after them. Bullets are flying and whining through the alley. One of the guys carrying a satchel drops, with the top of his head blasted clear away.

Another robber drops to his knees and starts firing. He hits the guard in the chest, and the guard drops on top of some cans. The gunman starts running for the satchel his pal has dropped, but the guard ain't finished. He's laying out flat on his stomach, but he pulls the trigger two times, missing. It's enough to make the robber give up any plans for the satchel and take off.

I watch it all, as though it's taking place in slow motion, like some kind of dream. Then it all gets clear. There's been a bank holdup. Four men had come running out of the bank. The bank guard had killed one of them, had himself been shot through the chest, and there's a satchel holding bank money just laying out there in the alley with nobody watching it.

It's enough for me. I run down the stairs and yank the back door open. The satchel ain't more than twenty feet away. The bank guard is stretched out with his face buried in a pile of rubble. I watch him all the time I'm running to the satchel, and he doesn't lift his head once. The guy he's shot is dead.

I grab the satchel and run back toward the doorway of my building, and unexpectedly two bullets ricochet off the wall next to my head. I catch a quick look. It's the guy in the lumber jacket, and I dive into the doorway as he fires more bullets my way.

Through the glass in the door I see one of the bank's employees jump out of the bank and he's firing at the man in the lumber jacket. I don't stick around to find out how things are going to work out. As I hit the stairs I hear an engine roaring and tires burning rubber. I run up the stairs to my room, drop the satchel on the bed and look out the window.

There's people out there now, kneeling next to the bank guard. Somebody's shouting, "Get an ambulance!" There's the still body of the dead robber, and the man in the lumber jacket ain't in sight.

I duck into the hall, scoot down the hallway to an old storage room that holds some sooty mattresses and unassembled beds. I jam the satchel in behind a mattress and go back to my room.

Now there's an army of cops out in the alley, and a sergeant's talking to old man Snelska, the landlord. Snelska's pointing at my window and it's enough to scare hell out of me, because all of a sudden I see him, the sergeant and two cops walking toward the doorway downstairs.

It comes to me quick then. I lock my door, strip, get into

my pajamas. I drink a water glass of rye, spill some into my hands and muss my hair with it. Then I get into bed.

The cops rap on my door seconds later and one of them is shouting, "Open up! Police!"

I take my time answering, then open the door like a lush who's been wrenched out of bed in the middle of the night. There's the sergeant with a red, angry puss, two cops and old man Snelska in the hall.

"What's going on? What's the idea banging on my door like that?" I say like I'm half shot, but inside I'm jumping.

"The bank's been robbed," old man Snelska hollers.

"No fooling?" I say. "You're kidding."

"Who kids about something like that? There's a stiff out in the alley and the bank's out fifty grand," Snelska says, all excited.

"Your window overlooks the alley," the sergeant says. "Did you see anything?" He sniffs and catches a whiff of the rye.

"Nothing. I been sleeping. Didn't hear a thing."

One of the cops grins. The sergeant mutters something under his breath, then says, "Go back to bed and sleep it off, bud."

"Thanks a lot for nothing." I tell him as he walks off. "Who asked you guys to come around and wake me up anyway? Huh?" I slam the door shut and lock it.

I got dressed again, went to the storeroom and counted the money. There was thirty thousand dollars. I put it back, stuffed the satchel behind the mattress and went back to my room. Everything was clear in my brain. I had more than enough money to marry Selma. She wanted fifteen and I came up with thirty. Talk about initiative.

One of the robbers had spotted me, but I had a strong feeling that he'd be mighty busy for a while trying to protect his own skin. I got into bed, put my hands behind my head and laughed for five minutes. I had it made. Selma would be discharged in two months. Life was going to be great.

I tried to call, couldn't reach her, and walked around on a cloud for the rest of the day. Later, I took a hundred dollars from the satchel and went out for a fine seafood dinner.

When I got back to my place, the dream came to an

end. There was a car parked across the street, with three men facing the front entrance of the building. I recognized the man who'd been wearing the lumber jacket; no lumber jacket now, but I recognized his face.

I almost panicked and ran, but forced myself to walk slowly around the corner. Then I went into the alley, got into the building using the rear entrance, and went to my room. I locked the door and stood in the darkness, trembling all over. All I wanted now was to get my hands on the money and take off. There was enough for a fast car or a plane ticket, but I had to move quickly.

I reached for the lock, but a knock at the door raised the hackles on my neck. I had a mental picture of the man in the lumber jacket standing out in the hall with a gun in his hand, waiting to kill me. It was like a bad dream. I stood frozen.

"Harold," a voice said on the other side of the door. It was Snelska, the landlord, but I jumped anyway. "I heard you running up the stairs, Harold," he said.

I switched on the light and opened the door.

He blinked. "What's the matter with you? Why are you standing in the dark? There was a man around to see you. He didn't know your name, but he described you and said he had a job for you."

I felt sick. "Did you give him my name?" I asked.

"Yeah, sure. I know you need a job."

"Thanks," I said. "Thanks a lot," and I shut the door.

Now I know I've got real big trouble. It ain't only the money they're after. I'm a witness to the crime; the bank guard is in critical shape over at the hospital; and it figures that those guys out in the car want to knock me off pronto.

Like I was saying before, I'm a good-looking guy with lots of brains, but I'm beginning to think I need some advice. For advice I have to go to a smart guy, and right away I think of Hot Rod Washburne.

I sneak downstairs to the hall phone and give him a buzz and tell him that I got trouble. I've known him a long time and he's a friend, so I tell him everything. He's so quiet while I'm talking that I think he's hung up, but he ain't. He's just listening and concentrating.

I say, "Washburne, you there?"

"Talk," he said. "Get on with it, you clod."

So I do, and I wind up by telling him that the robbers are parked right across the street in a big car. "There's three of them and they're ready to kill me."

"How much is in the satchel?"

"Thirty thousand."

"Hmm," he says. "I'll extricate you from your predicament, but the fee will be fifteen thousand dollars."

Hot Rod speaks real fancy, but I understand fifteen thousand dollars. That's half of thirty thousand dollars. There ain't nothing wrong with my figuring. "That's half," I holler.

"Well, suit yourself, my good man," says Hot Rod. "It's either fifteen thousand or else die."

Well, when he puts it that way, what choice do I have? "All right," I say.

"I've already formulated a plan. It's foolproof if you follow it to the letter. First, you wait at a window overlooking the street, until you see me double park in front of the hotel, then you get the satchel, come downstairs and jump into my car. I'll take care of the rest."

"I don't think you understand, Hot Rod. Those boys with the big guns are sitting across the street ready to shoot me down."

"I am tired, tired, do you hear?" Hod Rod says. "Why must I listen to this eternal barrage of doubt? I'm tired of the disbelievers. Do you or do you not want to make your escape with fifteen thousand dollars and your life? I am contemptuous of all those who will not believe."

Well, when he starts talking like that, right away I feel much better. I'm telling you Hot Rod is a very smart guy. "Okay," I say. "I'll be looking for you."

"Fifteen minutes, dolt," he says, and hangs up.

Let me tell you it's a long fifteen minutes before I see his little red sports car pull up before the hotel. I can also see those crooks across the street, and I'm almost ready to call the whole thing off but I know it's too late. Besides, Hot Rod Washburne is my ideal, thirty-eight and ain't worked a day in his life. You got to have faith in people. I get the satchel and go downstairs with it.

When Hot Rod sees me coming, he opens the car door for me, and I make a fast dash and jump in. I can see the crooks in the car across the street pointing their fingers at me, and their eyes are bugging right out of their heads.

Then Hot Rod says, "Now smile at them and wave good-by like they're your friends."

I think Hot Rod is cracking up, but I don't have any choice, so I give them a big grin and a wave. It shakes them up real bad. It looks like they're arguing. Then Hot Rod slides his World War One pilot glasses down over his eyes, guns the engine, and we take off.

I kind of figure that this is the end of the trail, when I see those crooks take out after us. They're close enough now so that I can see them and they look like they're snarling. It looks bad.

They're not too far behind while we drive out of town and then Hot Rod turns onto the state highway. The crooks start to close in, but Hot Rod's looking in his side mirror and he don't seem worried. In fact, he's humming happily, like he's already counting his fifteen thousand dollars.

We're climbing a mountain now and the crooks stay right where they are, not gaining.

"Harold, my boy," Hot Rod says, "did I ever tell you that I attended the university? It was the closest I ever came to work. Frightening experience, that."

"Yeah, I knew you went away for a while."

"That's where I was, my boy, studying at one of our seats of higher learning."

"Is that so?"

"Indeed. At the university there was a study made as to why so many of the good citizens of this country are mangled in automobile accidents."

We're near the top of the mountain now and I'm getting a little nervous. I say, "Hot Rod, those guys are closing in."

"Exactly," he says, as we got to the top of the mountain.

There's a sign that says: "All trucks use low gear on the descent." Hot Rod gunned the engine and we began to descend the mountain.

I say, "Hey, Hot Rod, there's a guy hanging out the front window aiming his gun at us."

Hot Rod sighs, like he is tired. "Confounded idiots! We will have to lose them, that's all there is to it," and he hits the accelerator.

I notice the speed then, because we're really flying down the side of the mountain. Below there's nothing except blackness and rocks. We're whipping around curves now.

"Hey, Hot Rod, maybe we ought to lose those guys some other place."

I look back and see that they're almost on our tail. A bullet goes whizzing by.

"Brazen nerve," Hot Rod says, and pours on the coal.

I figure, *So long, kid, so long fifteen grand, and so long, Hot Rod.*

I say, "Hot Rod, take it easy. There's a bad curve up ahead."

"You see that, do you, clod?"

And then, as we go into the turn, he gears down to low and floors the accelerator. The engine sounds as though it's going to explode and the car sways like it's going to flip, but it holds the road. The rear tires grab with all that extra power Hot Rod is putting on the wheels. He brakes hard and we look back.

Behind us the big car comes into the turn at high speed, with the brakes locked and the front wheels turned hard to the right. Only those crooks ain't going to the right. They're going straight ahead and they're still arguing. They go through the steel cable fence like it was never there. I count to five and there's a big booming noise at the bottom of the mountain. The sky gets a little lighter when the car starts burning.

Hot Rod pushes the clutch in and we drive slowly down the mountain. "It's all a matter of centrifugal force, my boy," Hot Rod explains. "A matter of applying low-gear power at the proper moment going into the turn, as opposed to applying brakes, which will do absolutely nothing to overcome centrifugal force."

I don't know what he's talking about, but it don't make any difference. I give him his fifteen thousand dollars, then I put in a call to Selma at the base.

The Wave at the switchboard tells me that Selma went and got married to a Navy cook.

You never know how those things are going to work out. Here I am with the fifteen thousand dollars all ready. I guess she got tired of waiting.

NOT EXACTLY LOVE

Fletcher Flora

Staring out the high casement window, open to the late afternoon, Marcus could see for miles across the wide river valley beyond the clustered multicolored roofs of suburban homes. He could see in the valley, besides a shining silver fragment of the river itself, a remote and casual pattern of farms and fields in the reds and browns and tenacious greens of autumn. It was a pretty sight, inviting and comforting to the eye, and he would have liked, had it been possible, to stand and view it at his leisure for the good of his soul. But it was not possible. At his feet, on the floor of the small room in which he stood, a room with only three walls, was another sight which neither invited nor comforted. It was the body of a girl, and the girl was dead, and she had priority, however reluctantly granted, over rivers and fields and farms in the tag end of a year that was not yet dead, but only dying.

With a soft sigh, barely audible to Sergeant Bobo Fuller in the shadows behind him, he lowered his eyes and sank slowly to one knee. The girl was lying face down, her head turned on the dark green composition floor to expose the left profile of a face in which death had left the blind eyes open and the lips turned back in a snarl of anger or pain or ultimate effort. Her feet pointed toward the open side of the room in which Fuller stood, her body tangential to a metal desk fastened to one wall of the room and supported on the opposite side by a pair of slender steel legs. Her arms were flung out ahead of her, the fingers of the small hands curved like claws, as if, in the instant of dying, she had desperately sought a hold on the smooth surface to prevent herself from being carried away by whatever dark angels had come for her.

Well, the angels had won, and she had lost, and so, thought Marcus, had he. He had been left with what was left of her, which wasn't much to leave in a world so fair with colored farms, and it was, after all, his own fault for being what he was. With his fingers, he probed among the short fair hairs of her head, finding the pulpy spot behind the crown, feeling with fastidious distaste the slight and sticky seepage on the fingertips. He stood up, sighing softly again. At the metal desk, really nothing more than a simple working surface, a single straight chair, also metal, was pushed neatly into place, its seat entirely beneath the surface, its back touching the edge. There were no books, no papers, nothing at all on the desk.

"She was struck from behind with something smooth and heavy," Marcus said. "What was it?"

In the shadows, Sergeant Bobo Fuller stirred and stepped forward. He did not like Marcus, who was blandly aware of the dislike, and he took a perverse satisfaction in speaking only when spoken to, and in contributing only what was specifically requested or routinely expected. As for Marcus, he did not share Fuller's animus, which he usually found amusing. In fact, he found Fuller rather stimulating, a constant challenge to perform at his best. Otherwise, he would have done what Fuller apparently wanted him to do. He would have asked for another partner to share his work, allowing Fuller to serve elsewhere with someone more compatible.

"We haven't found it," Fuller said. "It must have been hidden or carried away. We'll keep on looking, of course."

"Six tiers. Tens of thousands of books on more than a thousand shelves. It might have been hidden behind any of them. You've got a job, Fuller."

"If it's here, we'll find it."

"It probably isn't. Good luck, anyhow."

Marcus stepped back, his eyes moving about the tiny room with an effect of casualness, almost of indifference, stopping on the tour briefly, just once, when they reached the open casement window and the far-off colored pattern beyond.

"Abby Randal," he said. "Is that what you said her name was?"

"That's right. Abby for Abigail."

"I'd guess she's been dead about an hour. You agree?"

"That's close enough."

"I wonder where her books and papers are?"

"Books and papers? What makes you think she had any?"

"Well, these little rooms or carrels at the rear of each tier of the stacks are to study in. Ordinarily, you need books and paper to study. Books, at least. I wonder where they are."

"It strikes me that you could use these rooms for other things besides studying, if you wanted to. What I have in mind doesn't require any books."

"You have a naughty mind, Fuller, and so have I. Lover's quarrel, you think?"

"I wouldn't say so. Since you ask, one lover doesn't crack another lover over the head. Not in my opinion. What I mean is, it's not exactly an act of love."

"Quondam lovers, then. A not-so-tender parting. Jealousy sometimes becomes malevolent, Fuller."

There he went again. Showing off, as usual. What the hell did "quondam" mean? Well, Fuller wasn't about to ask, and he could, anyhow, being no fool, guess pretty accurately from the context. Former lovers? Was that what Marcus meant? If it was, why didn't he say so?

"Could be," Fuller said.

"Well, I'd better clear out of here now so the crew can get in. Not, probably, that they'll learn anything we don't already know, which isn't much. They ought to be here any minute. You've done a good job, Fuller. Everything under control."

It was praise deserved, and Fuller should have appreciated it, but he didn't. In fact, he resented it. He had come out alone in response to a call, and he had done what was necessary before Marcus arrived later, and it was, in his opinion, a deliberate and subtle kind of insult to imply that he might have done less.

"Thanks," he said. "I'll wait here for the crew."

"Right."

Marcus moved past him into a narrow cross-aisle running parallel to the row of small study rooms. From his position, he could look straight up one of the several perpendicular aisles between shelves of books that rose to the low ceiling of the tier on which he was. He was, in fact, on tier C of the library of the university located on the west edge of the city in which he, Detective-Lieutenant Joseph Marcus, earned his bread and credits toward his pension. The tier had been declared off-limits temporarily. Except for the lights burning in the aisle up which Marcus looked, no lights burned at all.

"Let me see if I've got it straight," Marcus said. "The head librarian's name is Henry Busch. The girl who found the body is Lena Hayes. The young man who was at the charging desk this afternoon is Lonnie Beckett. Straight?"

"Straight. I told them to wait in the librarian's office. It's on the next floor, two tiers up. You'll find them there."

"I'll go and see. Carry on, Fuller."

Carrying on, so far as Fuller could see, was for the present nothing more than waiting where he was in the capacity of a watchdog, and this is what he did, moving for the purpose to the casement window, where he looked out across the valley with a somewhat jaundiced eye that impaired his appreciation. Marcus, meanwhile, walked down the lighted aisle and up two short flights of steel stairs, turning to his right through an exit that brought him out into a large room with a high ceiling. He could see, looking straight ahead across an open area, into another room which was furnished with long tables, six chairs to a table, and a multitude of reference books on shelves around the walls. Immediately to his right was an enclosure bounded on two sides by a high counter, the charging desk, and on the other sides by two walls. Directly ahead of him, spanning the distance between the charging desk and another wall, was a low wooden fence with a gate in it. The gate locked automatically when closed, and the lock, electrically operated, could be released only if the person on duty at the charging desk could be induced to press a certain button. This, of course, was to prevent the invasion of the stacks by any person who could not produce a stack permit. Marcus had no permit, but he was privileged. He waited at the gate until a buzzing sound told him that the button was being pressed, and he escaped with an exorbitant feeling of freedom into the greener pasture on the other side of the fence.

In the librarian's office, he found the three that Fuller had promised. Henry Busch was a tall, slender man with streaks of gray in smooth, dark hair. The streaks had an artificial look, as if he had carefully contrived them for effect, but his thin, ascetic face and somber eyes, the latter looking out through thick lenses in heavy horn frames, did not lend credence to the suspicion. He was not a man, Marcus decided, to indulge his vanity with such nonsense. Lonnie Beckett, strangely, looked very much like a younger and slightly revised edition of Busch. Approximately the same height, same weight, same shape of head and face. His dark hair lacked the streaks, however; his eyes, the glasses. Lena Hayes was a looker. Marcus, who had somehow not expected such a pleasant surprise in a library, was pleasantly surprised. Her brown hair, thick and short and smoothly brushed, had the soft sheen of polished walnut in a lamplit room. She filled her sweater admirably, and her short skirt, after the fashion, was tailored to suggest a lean thigh and display a pretty leg. The bachelor's heart in Marcus's breast, which appreciated sights other than colored fields, began to swell. Whatever lovely Lena was studying in college, he thought, she could always make a living as an educated ecdysiast. And let Fuller look *that* one up in his Webster's.

"Mr. Busch?" Marcus said. "I'm Lieutenant Marcus. Or is it Doctor?"

"Small matter, small matter. As you choose." Busch came forward and offered his hand. "Come in, Lieutenant. We've been waiting for you."

"I know you have many things to do," Marcus said, accepting the hand. "I'll try not to detain you long."

"It's perfectly all right. We're at your disposal. This is Miss Lena Hayes, and this young man is Mr. Lonnie Beckett."

Marcus nodded at the pair in the order presented, resisting the temptation to linger on the former to the neglect of the latter.

"I understand," he said, "that you were all to some degree connected with the unfortunate occurrence in the stacks this afternoon."

"Not precisely," Busch said. "I am here only because I am the librarian and therefore responsible for what happens within my jurisdiction. It's a dreadful thing. Absolutely incredible."

"Whatever happens is credible," Marcus said reasonably. "However, perhaps we can settle the matter quickly without too much disturbance."

"Let us hope so, but I'm afraid there is not much help

that any of us can offer. That will be for you to decide, of course. I assume you wish to ask us some questions. We are prepared to cooperate fully, I assure you."

"Good. I can't ask for more." Marcus occupied a chair that had been placed for him, while Busch resumed his seat behind his desk. "To begin with, did any of you know the victim personally?"

"Speaking for myself only," Busch said, "I knew her casually. She was a graduate student, preparing a dissertation, and she was naturally often in the stacks doing reference work. She never asked for my personal assistance in any instance. I've spoken with her, exchanged some small talk, and that's all."

"Did you see her when she came to the library today?"

"I did not."

Marcus shifted his attention to Lonnie Beckett. "I understand that you were at the charging desk today when she entered the stacks. You must have admitted her."

"That's right. I did."

"Did she speak to you?"

"Yes. I didn't notice her when she came up, and she asked me to release the lock on the gate."

"Was she carrying anything? Any books or papers, I mean."

"I don't think so. No, I'm sure she wasn't. She always carried her materials in a briefcase, and she didn't have it with her. Now that I think of it, she wasn't even carrying a purse."

"Wasn't that a little odd? After all, students come to a library to study. They usually need certain materials, don't they?"

"Not necessarily. Maybe she just needed to do some reading from the shelves."

"I see. Then again, she may have come to meet someone. At any rate, deliberately or by chance, she *did* meet someone, and she was killed by whoever it was she met."

"Obviously."

The remark was innocent enough, a simple concession of a plain truth, but Marcus thought he detected in it a faint inflection of sarcasm. Not that his comment had deserved any better response; the plain truth rarely requires a commentary, especially when it is supported by a corpse. Still, he was not sure that he liked Lonnie Beckett. He felt that men in their middle twenties should show a certain amount of tenderness toward the senilities of men in their early forties. Even young men, he added sourly in his mind, who were too slick and assured by half. Aware of incipient prejudice, he would take care to lean the other way.

"As you say," he said, "obviously. I wonder if you would be good enough to answer my first question, which Mr. Busch has already answered for himself. Were you personally acquainted with Abby Randal?"

"I was." Lonnie Beckett leaned forward and rubbed his palms on his knees, as if they were sweating, and Marcus had the satisfaction of realizing that he was not, after all, quite so assured as he tried to appear. "I think it would be better if I were to explain our relationship now. I wouldn't want it to be exaggerated or misunderstood later, if it happened to come up."

"That's wise," said Marcus. "We always prefer to avoid misunderstandings if possible."

"Well, the truth is that I went out with Abby several times this last summer. We were both here for the summer session, that is, and we got acquainted and had a few dates."

"How many is a few?"

"Oh, I don't know. I didn't keep a record. Say a dozen."

"That's a nice, round number. What did you do on these dates?"

"Nothing much. We went to some shows downtown, a couple of dances. Mostly, we just strolled around the campus and talked about various things. She had a good brain and a sharp tongue. I thought she was fun to be with for a while, but eventually I lost interest."

"I imagine you can get to know a person pretty well just strolling around talking. What kind of person would you say she was?"

"Smart. I've said that. And tough. I mean tough in a complimentary sort of way. She was realistic, and she knew what she wanted, and I suspect that she didn't have many scruples about going after it. She came from a poor background, I think. She told me her parents were dead. I gathered she'd had to cut a lot of corners and shoot a lot of angles to get through college and into graduate school. She swore a lot, but you didn't seem to mind it, and hardly noticed it. I think it was part of her defenses, part of the toughness she'd had to develop in getting where she was.

Maybe I'm making her sound pretty crude, but she wasn't really. She was knowledgeable, and she had unexpected sensibilities and good taste in many areas. I guess you could call her genuine. She may have played rough when she needed to, but there was nothing phony about her."

"I think I get the picture. A smart, tough girl, basically honest but capable of making the most of her chances."

"That's about it."

"But not all of it. She was pretty, too. Even dead. I noticed that down in the stacks. Generally speaking, pretty girls get more chances than most."

"She was attractive enough, I suppose. Not my type, however."

Marcus had the sudden conviction that this remark was not intended for him alone. He had been vaguely disturbed all along, in fact, by a feeling that he was only ostensibly the primary audience in this matter. Lonnie Beckett was looking at him steadily as he talked, but he was talking to Lena Hayes. He was, in fact, repeating a confession. Marcus was sure of it, and he noticed for the first time, sneaking a quick glance, that Lena's ring finger was decorated with a small diamond. Her hands, lying in her lap, twitched and were still. Lifting his eyes briefly to her face, he saw that it was carefully composed in an expression of disdain, as if the summer's petty infidelities were of little or no importance. As indeed, Marcus thought, they weren't. Unless, he amended, they lead somehow to murder.

"Everyone to his own taste," he said. "Miss Hayes, how well did you know Abby Randal?"

"Hardly at all."

She did not say that this was well enough, but she managed to give the effect of saying it. The effect was achieved, at least in Marcus's ears, without the slightest inflection of scorn, and he willingly gave her points for composure, if not for compassion.

"You did, however, discover her body. It must have been quite a shock."

"It was not exactly a pleasant experience."

"What did you do when you discovered it?"

"I went immediately to the charging desk and told Lonnie. Lonnie went for Mr. Busch."

"You didn't scream?"

"I am not much given to screaming."

"I wondered if you attracted attention to your discovery. That's why I asked."

"No, not at all. I'm sure, even now, that only a few of us know what has happened. There was no one else on that level at the time, and Mr. Busch immediately made it off-limits to all students and personnel. Oh, a lot of people know that something is wrong, of course, but not exactly what."

"You seem to be a sensible young lady, Miss Hayes. I'm sure that the police appreciate it. Tell me, what was your purpose in going to that particular level at that time?"

"I wasn't going to that particular level. I was in the process of going to *all* levels. The lights in each aisle are controlled by a switch at the end. Students are supposed to switch them on when they need them and off when they leave. Only they often don't. Switch them off, I mean. I was going through the stacks doing it for them. I generally make two or three tours a day. We're on an economy kick."

"It seems to be catching. I take it, then, that you just happened to come across the body of Abby Randal in the course of your tour."

"Yes. I saw the body, and I acted just as I've told you."

"And you acted very well, I must say." Marcus turned again to Lonnie Beckett. "How long before the body was discovered had you been at the charging desk?"

"I came on duty at noon. That would make it about two hours."

"So it would. Can you tell me whom you admitted to the stacks in that time?"

"Oh, no." Lonnie Beckett shook his head, apparently appalled by the question. "I'm afraid that would be impossible."

"Impossible? Why? Do you mean there's a rule against telling?"

"No, nothing like that. It's just that I couldn't possibly be sure. Admitting a student is such a routine thing. If you recognize him, you press the button. If you don't recognize him, you glance at his permit and then press the button. I'm always busy, and I hardly notice the person I admit, let alone remember him. I mean, I could give you a long list of those who regularly enter the stacks, one day or another, but not of those who definitely entered this afternoon."

"You remembered Abby Randal, didn't you? You even remembered that she wasn't carrying a briefcase or purse."

"That's only because of what happened to her. If nothing had happened, I couldn't be sure right now if she'd been in this afternoon or not. Maybe, if I try, I can be reasonably certain about a few people, but I wouldn't have the least notion of the times they came and left."

"Do you remember the time when Abby Randal arrived?"

"No. If I guessed, I might be thirty minutes off."

"You're not much help."

"I'm sorry."

"Well, if you happen to be certain about something all of a sudden, make a note of it." Marcus abruptly returned full cycle to his starting point, which was Henry Busch. "Are there any other entrances to the stacks?"

"Yes. Certainly. At least one on each floor of the building, besides an outside door leading to the drive in the rear."

"Could anyone have entered the stacks this afternoon through one of those entrances?"

"It's possible, I suppose, but improbable. It's the policy to keep them locked at all times. The only ones who use them regularly are library personnel who have keys."

"Then any of the personnel could have entered through one of them?"

"Yes." This question brought a fleeting expression of fastidious distaste to the librarian's thin face, as if he found the implication both untenable and presumptuous. "Anyone, as I said, who had a key."

"Can these doors be opened from inside without a key?"

"They can. Each is equipped with a bar. When the bar is depressed, the lock is released."

"In that case, at least, they are all possible exits. The murderer could have left the stacks through any one of them."

"That's true."

"Well, that's just fine. There's nothing like having plenty of complications." Marcus stood up abruptly and slapped his thigh, apparently out of patience with the whole difficult and sordid affair. "I guess I'd better get out of here and let you go back to work. Before I go, however, I'd like to know where Abby Randal lived. Do you have a student directory or something like that?"

"The new one hasn't been issued yet." Henry Busch turned to Lonnie Beckett. "It seems that you were keeping company with Miss Randal this past summer, Lonnie. Perhaps you can tell the lieutenant her address."

"She was living in a room at 812 Morgan Street at the time," Lonnie said. "She may live there still. I wouldn't know about that."

He was talking to Lena Hayes again. All current knowledge disclaimed. The summer interlude over and done with, incredible and regretted in the bright chill air of autumn. Please, darling, can't we forgive and forget? Marcus couldn't say. He could only make a note of the address and say good-by.

He went down through the stacks again and saw Fuller on the way. The medical examiner had been and gone, and Abby Randal, in a basket, was about to go. A couple of technicians were completing a routine that would probably gain them nothing. Leaving Fuller to wind things up, he descended through the stacks to a lower level, where he used the outside door and went out past the police ambulance in the concrete drive.

He walked around the library, climbing a flight of steep steps up the slope on which the building stood, and so back to his car in the street. In his car he drove slowly off the campus and found Morgan Street, on which, in short order, he found 812. The house was a two-story frame structure that had been painted white at some remote time. There was a high front porch that Marcus crossed to reach the front door. The landlady, who responded after a while to his ringing, was an elderly woman with the sad, depleted air of one who was expiring slowly and interminably with a diminishing whisper of life through a slow leak. She was, Marcus guessed, one of the many widows near the campus who supplemented social security by renting rooms to students.

After identifying himself, Marcus asked for permission to examine Abby Randal's room, and the landlady, after expressing proper shock at what might be an improper request, demanded firmly to know the reason for it. Marcus had no objection to telling her what would soon be general knowledge, and he did so, thereby intensifying her shock to such a degree that he feared for a moment that social security was about to lose an obligation. She recovered sufficiently, however, to accompany him upstairs. She stood in the doorway, leaning for support against the jamb, while Marcus examined the room and went through its late occupant's effects.

He might have saved himself the trouble. There was a meager wardrobe hanging in the closet, a pair of heels and a pair of flats on the floor beneath. There was a bookcase packed with good books, mostly quality paperbacks, and on the walls, incompatible with a faded background of printed paper, there were two tolerable copies of two excellent paintings. There had been nothing wrong with Abby Randal's taste, but she had clearly lacked the funds to pamper it. There were no letters, not a single one. Apparently she had not only been an orphan, as Lonnie Beckett had said, but also lacking in friends. Or the friends didn't write. Or, if they wrote, Abby had not kept their letters. There was nothing, in brief, to indicate who she really was, or who might have had reason to kill her. In the top drawer of a dresser Marcus came across twenty-three dollars, and he wondered where she got her money. Well, she probably worked for it, and that was something he might need to pursue. In the meanwhile, he was able to assign her a certain character. A pretty girl. A smart, tough girl. A poor girl with a taste for quality.

"Who were her friends?" he asked. "Did she have many?"

"Not many." The landlady was still breathing rather heavily from the excitement or the climb up the stairs or both. "She was pleasant enough with the three other girls who live here, but not what you'd call friendly. Last summer she went out with a young man, but I think that's finished. She told me his name was Beckett, Lonnie Beckett. That's all I know about, except for Mr. Carrol," she added.

"Carrol? Who's he?"

"Richard Carrol, one of the teachers at the university. He's young, just an assistant, I think. Last summer he tutored Miss Randal in French. She was working on a dissertation, and she needed a reading knowledge to do some of her research."

"I see. Perhaps Mr. Carrol can give me a little more

information about Abby Randal. Do you know where I can find him?"

"Not offhand. He should be listed in the city directory if he has a telephone."

"Well, there's nothing more to be done here. Let's go look at the directory."

They descended the stairs, and the landlady switched on a light in the lower hall so Marcus could see the fine print in the directory. Locating the C's, he followed his finger to Carrol, Richard.

"Wymore Hall," he read aloud. "That's on campus, isn't it?"

"You might say so. It's just off it. It's reserved for bachelors on the faculty, but they take graduate students if there's any room for them after the faculty has been accommodated."

"You've been helpful." Marcus closed the directory and headed for the door. "Thanks very much."

"Glad to do what I could. That poor little Miss Randal! Poor little thing!"

Yes, thought Marcus, driving back toward the campus, poor little thing. He supposed that was an apt description of all that had been left of Abby Randal in the library stacks. It was beginning to get dark, and he drove with his lights on. Crossing the campus, he came to Wymore Hall on the other side. It was a long brick building of two stories. Within, beyond a foyer, was a small lounge where shaded lamps burned cozily. In the foyer, a young man was doing desk duty. Marcus reported.

"I'd like to see Mr. Carrol. Detective-Lieutenant Joseph Marcus calling."

The title worked its immediate magic, as he had anticipated. He was told to make himself comfortable in the lounge, and Mr. Carrol, who had lately returned, would be fetched at once. Marcus did as he was told, and approximately five minutes later Mr. Carrol appeared. He was a young man with pale blond hair, cropped close to a well-shaped skull, and candid blue eyes. His handgrip was firm.

"Lieutenant Marcus?" he said, not troubling to disguise a degree of natural apprehension. "I'm Richard Carrol. What can I do for you?"

"I'm making inquiries about a Miss Abby Randal,"

Marcus said. "There seems to be precious little known about her, and I thought you might be able to fill in with a few details."

"I'm afraid not. I know precious little about her myself."

"You tutored her in French this summer, didn't you?"

"That's correct. But French lessons are not particularly revealing. May I ask why you're interested in Abby?"

"She's been murdered."

"Holy smoke!" Richard Carrol's mouth gaped for a moment, and his blue eyes seemed to go briefly blind with sudden shock. "Where? When? How?"

"You have good news sense, Mr. Carrol." Marcus permitted himself a faint, humorless smile. "In the stacks at the library. This afternoon. By a blow on the head."

"What a shocking thing! I wish I could be of some help to you."

"Perhaps you can. We'll see. How often did you see Abby Randal this summer?"

"I saw her two evenings a week for approximately three months."

"That's quite a while. You surely must have learned something about her in that time."

"Not much. She was bright and learned readily, but I don't suppose that's particularly significant."

"Not particularly. Where did you meet for her lessons?" I asked.

"Oh, various places. The sessions were quite informal. Sometimes we used a study room in the library. Sometimes we found a bench on the campus. A few times we combined business and beer at one or another of the campus joints."

"I see. And she never confided in you? Not even over the beers?"

"Never. We kept things quite impersonal."

"Too bad. I was in hopes that the student-teacher relationship had developed a bit of sentiment. Sometimes it does, I understand."

"Not ours. Sorry to disappoint you."

"Well, I'm no stranger to disappointment. I meet it often."

A horn sounded outside, and Richard Carrol, hearing it, cocked his head. To Marcus, it sounded like just another horn on another automobile, but to Carrol it apparently had a distinctive character.

"There's my fiancée," he said. "She was to pick me up at this time. We're going out to early dinner. Perhaps you know of her. Her father's quite a prominent figure in the state. Member of the Board of Regents, for one thing. Leonard Manning, *the* Manning."

Marcus was properly impressed. Member of the Board of Regents was among the least of it. Among the most were umpteen million dollars and a ring in the governor's nose. A common cop couldn't help being impressed. Marcus guessed, sourly, that Richard Carrol had not been entirely unaware of this when he dropped the name. Not, of course, that you could blame him for wanting to make the most of a good thing. A Manning chick would be quite a catch for an assistant professor, involving the effect of an astronomical jump of brackets on 15 April. Lucky boy. Lucky, lucky boy. If things went well, *he* would never need to work thirty years for a pension.

"I've heard of him," Marcus said. "If you're ready to leave, I'll walk out with you."

"I'm truly sorry to have to run. Sorry, too, that I wasn't more helpful. I'll put my mind to it, however, and see if I can recall anything Abby said, anything at all, that you might find useful."

"Thanks. I'd appreciate it if you would."

They walked out together to the curb, where Marcus veered off toward his own car. The dome light was on in the expensive job waiting for Richard Carrol, and Marcus could see the Manning girl behind the wheel digging for something in her purse. The sight gave him a perverse sense of satisfaction. She might have her little fist in her old man's bottomless pocket up to the elbow, he thought, but she could never get within a thousand miles of Atlantic City when looks was buying the ticket. It was somehow comforting to know that you can have so much without quite having it all.

So comforted, Marcus drove downtown to headquarters. He made some notes, wrote a report, and went out to eat. Having eaten and being off duty, he stopped in a congenial bar and drank three beers and watched *Burke's Law* on TV. He liked to watch it because Amos Burke made it look so easy. Marcus didn't resent this. His envy had a quality of congeniality that was in accord with the bar and the beers. After Amos solved his case, Marcus took his own case home, still unsolved, and went to bed with it.

The next morning at headquarters, he was trapped at his desk for a couple of hours, after which he spent another half-hour briefing the Chief. Returning to his desk to snatch his hat and make his escape, he was caught in the act by the medical examiner, a skinny little man with the dyspeptic expression of one who suffered a chronic affliction of either cynicism or gas. He seemed so physically frail as to be threatened by every draught, but he was, in fact, as tough as a strand of baling wire. At the moment, in any event, he was securely anchored in Marcus' spare chair.

"I usually just write it in a report," he said, "but this time I thought I'd hog all the fun of telling you personally."

"Enjoy yourself," Marcus said. "Of telling me what?"

"Cursory examination of your latest little victim reveals that she suffered from a well-known physical condition that is sometimes a problem, but seldom fatal. She had round heels."

"Oh?" Marcus sank into his chair and leaned back. "Are you positive?"

"Certainly I'm positive. The condition is easily diagnosed when it's supported by a severe case of pregnancy."

"I got the point, Doc. How long pregnant?"

"About three months."

"Odd. Very odd." Marcus closed his eyes, apparently preparing to catch forty winks. "I've been building a picture in my mind, and somehow I had her figured as too tough and too smart to get caught that way."

"You'd better start over."

"Maybe so. Maybe not. Maybe there's an angle I missed."

"Such as?"

"Such as maybe she was tough enough and smart enough to arrange things deliberately."

"You're guessing. That's the trouble with you fancy cops. Someone gives you a scientific fact and you use it as a gimmick in a fairy tale. Anyhow, if you're right, the arrangement didn't turn out to be very smart. Fatal is how it turned out."

"Now you're the one who's guessing. How do you know it was the motive for her murder?"

"Come off, Marcus. It'll do until a better one turns up."

"Well, that's no guess. That's the truth if I ever heard it." Marcus suddenly got up and grabbed his hat. "I've got to run, Doc. Thanks for your brilliant diagnosis. I didn't think you had it in you."

He escaped into the hall, leaving the old medic to swallow his sour retort, and twenty minutes later he was climbing the steps to the entrance of the university library. Inside, he continued to climb, coming out on the floor in front of the charging desk. Lonnie Beckett was on duty behind the desk. He greeted Marcus courteously but with less than enthusiasm.

"Good morning, Lieutenant," he said dryly. "Looking for someone?"

"I was hoping to find Miss Hayes here. There's something I want to clear up with her."

"Lena's in class." Lonnie consulted the watch on his right wrist. "She'll be out in about six minutes."

"Where does the class meet?"

"Grover Hall. That's the stone building just around the curve in the street out front. But maybe I can tell you what you want to know."

"I don't think you can. There's something else, though. You told me yesterday afternoon that Abby Randal was tough and smart, but that wasn't all of it. Why didn't you tell me that she was also capable of excessive generosity?"

"I don't know what you mean. Generous with what? I told you she was hard up. She didn't have much with which to be generous."

"All girls have something. As my friend Fuller would say, it's not exactly love. Sometimes it passes for love."

Lonnie Beckett's thin face was drained and pinched. His lower lip began to quiver, and he sucked it in between his teeth and held it for several seconds. Marcus watched him with a kind of clinical curiosity, as if his interest were purely academic.

"I don't believe it," Lonnie said finally. "Abby wasn't like that at all."

"No? Well, maybe not. Maybe she discovered some other way of getting pregnant. Not, you understand, that I don't respect you for trying to protect a girl's reputation. Incidentally, I noticed yesterday that Miss Hayes was wearing a diamond on her ring finger. I had a notion that you put it there."

"All right. So I did."

"Congratulations. Let's hope she leaves it where you put it."

Turning away, Marcus descended the stairs, left the building, and walked along the curving walk to Grover Hall. There was a stone bench beside the walk, and he sat down on it in the pale, cold sunlight. He lit a cigarette and waited, drawing the collar of his coat around his neck. He should have worn an overcoat. The campus was almost deserted at the moment, the students captives in half a thousand classes, but soon afterward it was swarming with them during a brief intermission in their captivity. Marcus watched them closely, searching for Lena Hayes, but he was disconsolately aware that it would be a minor miracle if he could pick her out of this mob dispersing rapidly in all directions. Luck was with him, however, and there she was, coming briskly along the walk on what was clearly a tight schedule. He waited until she came abreast, and then he stood up, touching his hat.

"Hello, Miss Hayes," he said.

"Oh, Lieutenant Marcus." She stopped, facing him, but impatient to be on her way again. "I'm sorry I haven't any time right now. I have another class."

"That's all right. I'll just walk along with you if you don't mind."

"Can't it wait, whatever you want to see me about? I'll be free in another hour."

"I'll try not to make you late for your class. Could I carry your books?"

"No, thank you."

She started off down the walk again, and Marcus fell in beside her. He wished wistfully that she would let him carry the books. It had been a long, long time since he had performed such a service for a girl so lovely.

"You told me yesterday," he said, "that you were switching off lights in the stacks when you discovered Abby Randal's body. Where are the switches located? At which end of the shelves, I mean."

"There are switches at both ends."

"Which were you using?"

"The ones nearer the stairs, naturally. Why should I walk all the way to the other end and then back to the stairs again when I was ready to go to the next level?"

"But that is exactly what you did, Miss Hayes; at least in one instance. Otherwise, you couldn't possibly have seen Abby Randal's body on the floor of that little room at the far end. Isn't that correct?"

"Of course not. I went back there for a perfectly good reason. When I reached the aisle that ends just opposite the door of the room, the lights were off, as they should have been, but I happened to notice a book on the floor near my end of the aisle. I switched on the lights so that I could see to put the book back on the shelf where it belonged, and then I saw that several books were on the floor all the way along the aisle. It looked as if someone had pulled them off the shelves maliciously just to make extra work. Anyhow, I went down the aisle and replaced the books, and that's how I happened to get back where I could see the body."

"Tell me, Miss Hayes. Which shelf were the books from?"

"The bottom one, just off the floor."

"All of them?"

"Yes."

"Didn't you think that was odd?"

"Not at all. I merely thought it was devilish. The books are more difficult to replace on the low shelves. You have to sit on your heels to do it. If you're not careful, you pop your hose and start a run."

"You must have been rather annoyed."

"To put it bluntly, I was mad as hell. Then I discovered the body, of course, and it was all knocked right out of my head."

"I can appreciate that. Is this your building?"

"Yes. I'll have to rush, or I'll be late. Is that all you wanted to ask me?"

"That's all."

"I can't see that it makes any difference."

"It makes a great deal of difference. Thanks, Miss Hayes."

He watched her hurry up the walk to the building, filled with the ghosts of seasons past, and then he turned with a sigh and went back to his car. He sat for a while under the wheel. He was strangely reluctant to do what was left to be done, and he decided he would go back to headquarters and try to get Fuller to do it for him. Fuller probably wouldn't mind, inasmuch as it would give him a chance to play the lead for a while, and in the meantime he, Marcus, could prepare himself for the most depressing part of his job, which was charging people for things they never should have done. So deciding, he returned to headquarters and left word with the desk sergeant to send Fuller to him when Fuller turned up. It was almost an hour later when Fuller came in.

"If you're wondering whether we've found the weapon or not," Fuller said, "we haven't."

"Well, I wouldn't worry about it. It was probably a length of lead pipe or something that could be carried in a briefcase or under a coat. I wonder if you'll do me a favor?"

"I'll do anything," said Fuller carefully, "that's part of my job."

"You always do your job, Fuller."

"Thanks. What's the favor?"

"Run out to the university and bring in Abby Randal's murderer. No hurry, however. Whenever it's convenient."

Fuller's face turned slowly to stone. Deliberately, with an effect of great caution, he sat down in the spare chair and cupped his knees in the palms of his big hands. He spoke with dreadful restraint, staring at the wall above and beyond Marcus.

"Just like that. Go out and bring in Abby Randal's murderer, Fuller. At your convenience, Fuller." He lowered his eyes to his hands and turned the hands over on his knees, flexing the fingers. "Maybe you wouldn't mind telling me how you know all of a sudden who the murderer is?"

"That's easy, Fuller. I know because Abby Randal told me."

"Oh, that explains it, then. It was a simple matter of talking with a ghost. I've never had the privilege of talking with a ghost, myself. How come you always get to do the interesting things?"

"No ghost, Fuller. She told me before she died."

"Somehow I was under the impression that you never saw her before she died."

"So I didn't, Fuller, but she left the message."

"I'm just a dumb sergeant, I guess. I don't read very well.

I probably wouldn't have got the message if she'd written it in blood, of which there wasn't any, or in the dust on the floor, of which there also wasn't any."

"She wrote it in books, Fuller. We assumed in the beginning that she was killed in that little room where she was found, but she wasn't. She only went there to die. I had suspicions even in the beginning, because the chair was pushed neatly under the desk, as you'll remember. She obviously hadn't been there long enough to use the room, at any rate, but that didn't preclude the possibility of her being struck down as she entered. That's what the position of the body suggested. I learned this morning, however, that she was attacked at the far end of the aisle. The murderer should have struck her again and again to make sure that she was dead, but he was afraid to linger, of course, and hurried away. That was a mistake, because Abby Randal didn't die. Not immediately. She was tough. She was smart. Even dying, in pain and fear, she thought of a way to leave us the name of her murderer. She dragged herself down that aisle, all the way, pulling books off the bottom shelf to mark her path and let us know that there was a *reason* for what she was doing. When she got to that little room, she was where she wanted to go. She crawled in and died. Why? Why, Fuller?"

"I suppose," said Fuller with heavy sarcasm not unmixed with despair, "that she wanted to die in privacy."

"No. She crawled there because that was the one way she could name her murderer. Do you know what those little study rooms are called, Fuller? *They're called carrels.* There's a guy on the faculty out there whose name is Richard Carrol. He tutored Abby Randal in French last summer, and he had a lot to lose, name of Manning, from becoming a premature papa in collaboration with the wrong mama. He said his sessions with Abby were informal, and they must have been. And I'll give you odds, Fuller, that their last one was held yesterday afternoon in the library stacks."

"Is this all the evidence you've got? It may be true, but you'll have a hell of a time proving it."

"That's right. It's not enough for the district attorney to take to court. We'll find something else, though. It's not too hard to find circumstantial evidence when you know where to look for it. Anyhow, we won't really need it. I talked with Carrol last night, and I know the type. He'll break like an egg under pressure. But how in the devil can we get a confession if you won't bring him in?"

Fuller stood up. He shook his head as if to clear it of fog.

"If you can make it stick, it's great work," he said. "I've got to admit that."

"I'm not proud of it," Marcus said. "Abby Randal did all the work. I just came along later to grab the credit."

THE SWINGING SHERIFF

Ed Lacy

When the old car entered Harbor Bay (population 994), the small man sitting beside the driver asked, "Whatcha slowing down for, Buddy? You lost? Don't know why you borrowed this old heap when you got a big new car to ride around in. Don't seem right."

Buddy, a muscular giant in a worn sweatshirt and dungarees, his young face sullen and puffed, parked before the village's only liquor store as he said, "Knock off the chatter, Artie. I ain't lost, know what I'm doing. I been on edge the last couple days, too sharp. You go in and buy me a pint of the best bourbon." The giant had a high, raspy voice.

Thin face twisted with astonishment, Artie asked, "Buddy, you hear what your mouth is saying? You nuts?"

"Keep talking and I'll cool you, Artie. I mean it! Go buy the bottle, or do you want me to get it?"

Artie seemed about to say something but jumped out of the car instead of arguing. Buddy glanced around the tiny main street, suddenly cleared his throat, and spat.

A stocky, gray-haired man in a worn brown police uniform crossed to the car, said, "Against the law to spit on the streets here, stranger. Don't do it again."

Easing his big frame out of the car, Buddy stood in front of the sheriff, gave him a grin of crooked teeth, and repeated the offense.

The sheriff said slowly, "All right, enough of that. Come with me—there will be a fine."

Artie, coming out of the liquor store, rushed between the two large men, asked in a whisper, "Officer, you know who this is?"

"Yes: a man who's deliberately ignored a Harbor Bay ordinance. I'm taking him in."

"You can't do that—*he's Buddy Winston!*" Artie said.

Buddy grinned proudly, rasped, "It's okay, Artie. This store cop says he going to take me in—let him try it! This oughta be good."

The sheriff's thick hand rested on his holster. "You're coming with me—at gun point if necessary. Get moving!"

Artie wailed, "Buddy, please don't start nothing!"

The Harbor Bay jail, police station, post office, volunteer fire department, public toilet, and mayor's office were all in one ancient building. Artie had raced to the nearest phone and, within twenty minutes after he had made a call, the sheriff's office was besieged by phone calls from newspapers. An hour later reporters and photographers arrived by car and helicopter. The sheriff refused to see them.

Exactly ninety minutes after Buddy Winston had been placed in the jail's only cell, a car from the County District Attorney's office braked to a stop and a Mr. Smith pushed his way through the newsmen, into the sheriff's office. Mr. Smith's worried face and tropical suit were damp with sweat. He asked the sheriff, "Damn it, Al, what are you holding Buddy Winston for. Speeding?"

"He violated Harbor Bay Ordinance Three, Section One, and also for disorderly conduct and resisting arrest."

"Now listen to me, Al. You've read the papers. Buddy Winston is to fight for the heavyweight championship next week. The biggest gate in ring history is at stake, plus a two-million-dollar TV contract! All hell has broken out in the county seat, not to mention pressure from the state capital. Forget he was spitting on the street!"

"Why should I forget it, Mr. Smith? And I told you, I'm also booking him for disorderly conduct and resisting an officer."

"Al, use your head. There's a gang of reporters outside and if you hold Winston—even overnight—it will upset him, ruin the fight, ruin a three-million-dollar deal—and the Lord knows what else! Right this second the eyes of the world are on Harbor Bay!"

"Does being a big-shot pug make Winston above the law?" the sheriff asked calmly.

"Al, come on! Buddy was in prison several times before he turned to fighting—you've read the news stories about him—another rap will ruin him! You hold him and those reporters will roast Harbor Bay to a crisp, ruin your summer tourist trade!"

"All I know is a man broke the law."

"Al, for the love of . . . use your head, think fast! What are you going to tell those reporters—that because a man spit on your street you're going to spoil a three-million-buck business?"

"Mr. Smith, are you officially ordering me to release Buddy? That what you want me to tell the reporters?"

The D.A.'s man wiped his wet face. "Al, don't put words in my mouth. I'm here to help you. This story will be on the front page of every newspaper in the world—do you want to make the village look foolish? You *have* to see those reporters!"

Opening the door of his office, the sheriff stepped out into the crowded hallway to face a battery of flash guns. Questions were flung at him as he blinked, held up a big hand for silence.

In his slow voice he said, "Gentlemen, I have a statement to make. Harbor Bay is a peaceful village, and I've been its sheriff for going on twenty-five years. I guess most of you think I'm a hick cop out to make a name for myself. Well, I may be a hick and I certainly do value my name. These are the facts: I have arrested one Buddy Winston, a professional fighter, for breaking a village ordinance after he had been warned not to do it again, and for disorderly conduct and resisting arrest. I've been warned that if I hold him I'll ruin big business, the TV industry, and about bring the world to an end. As you must suspect, a great deal of pressure has been brought on me to release this man.

"I am fifty-two years old and my name has always been on the side of law and order. I don't intend to have my name tarnished now, be made an accessory to a fraud. If I release Buddy Winston—aside from the fact he broke the law—I would be perpetrating a three-million-dollar fraud on the American people. There's something you fellows don't know—when I took Buddy Winston in, he swung on me and I was forced to subdue him, knocked him out with my fist. Therefore I am *not* going to release him . . . for if a fifty-two-year-old man can flatten Mr. Winston, it would indeed be a fraud to allow this glass-jawed bum to fight for the heavyweight championship of the world!"

ONE ON A DESERT ISLAND

Donald E. Westlake

There is a perennial cartoon idea which begins, "Two men on a desert island. One of them says . . ." Then there is a funny gag line delivered by one of the men. It can be funny because there are two of them. But what about *one* man on a desert island?

Jim Kilbride was one man on a desert island. It was one of a group of four islands, alone in the middle of the Pacific, south of the major sea lanes. The island that Jim Kilbride was on was the largest of the four, a mile by a mile and a half. It was mainly unshaded sand, washed by the ocean during high tide, but there were two small hillocks near the center of the island, on which were stunted trees and dark green shrubbery. On the eastern side of the island there was a small, curving indentation in the beach, forming a natural cove in miniature, a pool surrounded by a half-circle of sand and a half-circle of ocean. A few birds soared among the islands, calling to each other in raucous voices. The caws of the birds and the whisper of the surf against the beach were the only sounds in the world.

Jim Kilbride had happened to be on a desert island, alone, through a series of half-understood desires and strange events. He had once been a bookkeeper, snug and safe and land-locked, working for a small textile firm in San Francisco. He had been a bookkeeper, and he had looked like a bookkeeper. Short, under five foot seven. The blossomings of a paunch, although he was only twenty-eight. Hair straight and black and limp, with a round and receding forehead that shone beneath the office lights. Round eyes behind rounder spectacles, steel-framed and sliding down his nose. A tie that hung from his neck like the frayed end of a halter. Suits that had looked fine in the department-store window, on the tall and lean and confident mannequins.

He was James Kilbride then, and he wasn't happy. He wasn't happy because he was a cliché and he knew it. He lived with his mother, and he never went out with women, and he rarely drank intoxicants. When he read the sad tales of contemporary realism, about mild and unobtrusive bookkeepers who lived with their mothers and who never went out with women, he felt ashamed and unhappy, because he knew they were talking about him.

His mother died, and this is where all the sad tales begin or end, but for James Kilbride, nothing had changed. The office remained the same; the bus took no new routes. The house was larger, now, and darker and more silent, but that was all.

His mother had been well insured, and there was quite a bit left over. Something from his reading, or from a conversation over lunch, gave him the idea and the impetus, and he bought a boat. He bought a sailing cap. On Sundays, alone, he went sailing in the near waters of the Pacific.

But still nothing changed. The office was still bright with incandescent lights, and the bus took no new routes. He was still James Kilbride, and he still lay wide awake in bed and dreamed of women and another, livelier, happier sort of life.

The boat was a twelve-footer, with a tiny cabin. It was painted white, and named *Doreen,* the woman he had never met. And on one bright Sunday, when the ocean was bright and clean and the sky was scrubbed blue, he stood in his boat and stared out to sea, and he thought about going to China.

The idea grew. It took months, months of thought, of reading, of preparation, before he knew one day that he would go to China. He really and positively would. He would keep a diary and would publish it and become famous and meet Doreen.

He loaded the boat with canned food and water. He arranged for a leave of absence from his employer. For some reason, he couldn't bring himself to quit completely, though he intended to never come back. And then he took off, once again on a Sunday, and steered the little boat out to sea.

The Coast Guard intercepted him, and brought him back. They explained a variety of rules and regulations to him, none of which he understood. On the second try, they were more aggressive, and told him that a third attempt would result in a jail sentence.

The third time, he left at night, and he managed to slip through the net they had set for him. He thought of himself as a spy, a dark and terrible figure, fleeing ruthlessly through the muffled night from an enemy land.

By the third day, he was lost. He had no idea where he was or where he was going. He paced back and forth, his sailing cap protecting him from the sun, and stared out at the trembling surface of the sea.

Ships, black silhouettes, passed on the horizon. Islands were mounds of mist far, far away. The near world was blue and gold, and silence was broken only by the muted play of the wavelets around his boat.

On the eighth day, there was a storm, and this first storm he managed to survive intact. He bailed until the boat was dry, then slept for almost twenty-four hours.

Three days later, there was another storm, a fierce and outraged boiling of water and air, that came at dusk and poured foaming masses of black water across the struggling boat. The boat was torn from him, and he lashed his arms about in the water, fighting and clawing and swallowing huge gulps of the furious water.

He reached the island at night, borne by the waves into the slight protection of the crescent cove. He crawled up the sanded beach, above the reach of the waves, and slept.

When he awoke, the sun was high and the back of his neck was painfully burned. He had lost his sailing cap and both of his shoes. He crawled to his feet and moved inland, toward the scrubby trees, away from the burning sunlight.

He lived. He found berries, roots, plants that he could eat, and he learned how to come near the birds, as they sat preening themselves on the tree branches, and stun them with hurled stones. He was lucky, in one way. In his pocket were matches, water-proofed, that he had put there before the storm hit. He built a small shelter from bits of branch and bark. He scooped out earth to make a shallow bowl in the ground, and started a fire in it, keeping the fire going day and night. He only had eight matches.

He lived. For the first few days, the first few weeks, he kept himself occupied. He stared for hours out at the sea, waiting expectantly for the rescuers. He prowled the small island, until he knew its every foot of beach, its every weed and branch.

But rescuers didn't come, and soon he knew the island as well as he had once known the route of the bus. He started drawing pictures in the sand, profiles of men and women, drawings of the birds that flew and screeched above his head. He played tic-tac-toe with himself, but could never win a game. He had neither pencil nor paper, but he started his book, the book of his adventures, the book that would make him more than the minor clerk he had always been. He composed the book carefully, memorizing each sentence as he completed it, building it slowly and exactly, polishing each word, fashioning each paragraph. He had freedom and individuality and personality at last. He roamed the island, reciting the completed passages aloud.

It wasn't enough. It could never be enough. Months had passed, and he had never seen a ship, a plane, or any human face. He prowled the island, reciting the finished chapters of his book, but it wasn't enough. There was only one thing he could do, to make the new life bearable, and at last he did it.

He went mad.

He did it slowly; he did it gradually. For the first step, he postulated a Listener. No description, not even age or sex, merely a Listener. As he walked, speaking his sentences aloud, he made believe that someone walked beside him on his right, listening to him, smiling and nodding and applauding the excellence of his composition, pleased by Jim Kilbride, no longer the petty clerk.

He came almost to believe that the Listener really existed. At times, he would stop suddenly and turn to the right, meaning to explain a point he thought might be obscure, and he would be shocked, for just a second, to find that no one was there. But then he would remember, and laugh at his foolishness, and walk on, continuing to speak.

Slowly, the Listener took on dimension. Slowly, it became a woman, and then a young woman, who listened attentively and appreciatively to what he had to say. She still had no appearance, no particular hair color, shape of face, no voice, but he did give her a name, Doreen. Doreen Palmer, the woman he had never met, had always wanted to meet.

She grew more rapidly. He realized one day that she had honey-colored hair, rather long, and that it waved back gracefully from her head when the breeze blew across the island from the sea. It came to him that she had blue eyes, round and intelligent and possessing great depths, deeper even than the ocean. He understood that she was four inches shorter than he, five foot three, and that she had a sensuous but not overly voluptuous body and dressed in a white gown and green sandals. He knew that she was in love with him, because he was brave and strong and interesting.

But he still wasn't completely mad, not yet. Not until the day he first heard her voice.

It was a beautiful voice, clear and full and caressing. He had said, "A man alone is only half a man," and she replied, "you aren't alone."

In the first honeymoon of his insanity, life was buoyant and sweet. Over and over, he recited the completed chapters of his book to her, and she would interrupt, from time to time, to tell him how fine it was, to raise her head and kiss him, her honey-blonde hair falling about her shoulders, to squeeze his hand and tell him that she loved him. They never talked about his life before he had come to the island, the incandescent office and the ruled and rigid ledgers.

They walked together, and he showed her the island, every grain of sand, every branch of every tree, every bush and bird. He showed her how he killed the birds, and how he kept the fire going, because he only had eight matches. And when the infrequent storms came, whipping the island in their insensate rages, she huddled close to him in the lean-to he had built, her blonde hair soft against his cheek, her breath warm against his neck, and they would wait out the storm, their arms clasped tightly about each other, their eyes staring at the guttering fire, hoping and hoping that it wouldn't be blown out.

Twice it was, and he had to use precious matches to start it going again. But they reassured each other both times, saying that next time the fire would be more fully protected and would not go out.

One day, as he was talking to her, reciting the last chapter he had so far finished of the book, she said, "You haven't written any more in a long while. Not since I first came here."

He stopped, his train of thought broken, and realized that what she had said was true. He told her, "I will start the next chapter today."

"I love you," she answered.

But he couldn't seem to get the next chapter started. He didn't want to start another chapter, really. He wanted to recite for her the chapters he had already completed.

She insisted that he start a new chapter, and for the first time since she had come to join him, he left her. He walked away, to the other end of the island, and sat there, staring out at the ocean.

She came to him after a while and begged his forgiveness. She pleaded with him to recite the earlier chapters of the book once more, and finally he took her in his arms and forgave her.

But she brought the subject up again, and again, more sternly each time, until finally one day he snapped at her, "Don't nag me!" and she burst into tears.

They were getting on each other's nerves, he realized that, and he slowly came to realize, too, that Doreen was coming to behave more and more like his mother, the only woman he had ever really known. She was possessive, as his mother had been, never letting him alone for a minute, never letting him go off by himself so he could think in peace. And she was demanding, as his mother had been, insisting that he show ambition, that he return to work on the book. He almost felt she wanted him to be just a clerk again.

They argued violently, and one day he slapped her, as he had never dared to do to his mother. She looked shocked, and then she wept, and he apologized, kissing her hands, kissing her cheek where the red mark of his hand stood out like fire against her skin, running his fingers through the softness of her hair, and she told him, in a subdued voice, that she forgave him.

But things were never again the same. She became more and more shrewish, more and more demanding, more and more like his mother. She had even started to look something like his mother, a much younger version of his mother, particularly in her eyes, which had grown harder and less blue, and in her voice, which was higher now and more harsh.

He began to brood, to be secretive, to keep his thoughts to himself and to not speak to her for hours at a time. And when she would interrupt his thoughts, either to gently touch his hand as she had used to do or, more often now, to complain that he wasn't doing any work on his book, he would think of her bitterly as an invader, as an interloper, as a stranger. Bitterly, he would snap at her to leave him alone, to stay away from him, to leave him in peace. But she would never leave.

He wasn't sure when the thought of murder first came to his mind, but once there, it stayed. He tried to ignore it, tried to tell himself that he wasn't the type of person who committed murder. He was a bookkeeper, a small and mild and silent man, a calm and passive man.

But he wasn't that at all, not any more. He was an adventurer, a roamer of the sea, a dweller in the middle of the Pacific, envied by all the poor and pathetic bookkeepers in all the incandescent offices in the world. And he was, he knew now, quite capable of murder.

Day and night he thought about it, sitting before the tiny fire, staring into its flames and thinking about the death of Doreen. And she, not knowing his thoughts, not knowing how dangerous her actions were, continued to nag him, continued to demand that he work on the book. She took to watching the fire, snapping at him to bring more bark, more wood, not to let the fire go out as he had done the last two times, and he raged at the viciousness and unfairness of the charge. The storms had put the fire out, not he. But, she answered, the storm wouldn't have put the fire out had he paid it the proper attention.

Finally, he could stand it no longer. In their earlier, happier days, they had often gone swimming together, staying near the shore for fear of sharks and other dangerous animals that might be out in the deeper water. They hadn't swum together for a long time, and one day, casually and cunningly, he suggested that they take up the practice again.

She agreed at once, and they stripped together and ran into the water, laughing and splashing one another as though they were still lovers and still delighted with one another. He ducked her, as he had done in the old days, and she came up laughing and spluttering. He ducked her again, and this time he held her under. She fought him, when she realized his intentions, but he felt the new muscles in his arms grow taut, and he held her in a terrible grip, keeping her underwater until her struggles grew feebler and feebler and finally subsided. He then released her, and watched the ebb and flow of the waves carry her body out to sea, the honey-blonde hair swaying in the water, the blue eyes closed, the soft body lying limp in the water. He stumbled back to the beach, shaken and exhausted, and collapsed on the sand.

By the next day, he was feeling the first touches of remorse. Her voice came back to him, and her face, and he remembered the happiness of their early days together. He picked over the broken bones of all of their arguments, and now he could see so clearly the times when he, too, had been in the wrong. He thought back and he could see where he had treated her unfairly, where he had always thought only of himself. She, however, had wanted him to finish the book, not for her sake, but for his own. He had been short-tempered and brutal, and it had been his fault that the arguments had grown, that they had come to detest each other so much.

He thought about how readily and how happily she had agreed to go swimming with him, and he knew that she had taken it as a sign of their reconciliation.

As these thoughts came to him, he felt horrible anguish and remorse. She had been the only woman who had ever returned his love, who had ever seen more in him than a little man stooped over ledgers in a hushed office, and he had destroyed her.

He whispered her name, but she was gone, she was dead, and he had killed her. He sprawled on the sand and wept.

In the following weeks, although he missed her terribly, he grew resigned to the loss. He felt that something dramatic and of massive import had moved through his life, changing him forever. His conscience pained him for the murder, but it was a sweet pain.

Five months later, he was rescued. A small boat came to the island from a bulging gray steamer, and the sailors helped him as he climbed clumsily into the boat. They brought him to the steamer, and helped him up the Jacob's-ladder to the deck of the boat. They fed him, and gave him a place to sleep, and when he was refreshed, he was brought before the captain.

The captain, a small gray man in faded clothing, motioned to him to sit down in the chair near his desk. He said, "How long were you on the island?"

"I don't know."

"You were alone?" asked the captain gently. "All the time?"

"No," he said. "There was a woman with me. Doreen Palmer."

The captain was surprised. "Where is she?"

"She's dead." All at once, he started to weep, and the whole story came out. "We fought, we got on each other's nerves, and I murdered her. I drowned her and her body was washed out to sea."

The captain stared at him, not knowing what to do or say, and finally decided to do nothing, but simply to turn the man over to the authorities when they reached Seattle.

The Seattle police listened first to the captain's statement, and then they talked to Jim Kilbride. He admitted the murder at once, saying that his conscience had troubled him ever since. He spoke logically and sensibly, answering all their questions, filling in the details of his life on the island and the crime he had committed, and it never occurred to them that he might be mad. A stenographer typed his confession and he signed it.

Old office friends visited him in jail and looked at him with new interest. They had never known him, not really. He smiled and accepted their awe.

He was given a fair trial, with court-appointed counsel, and was found guilty of first-degree murder. He was calm and dignified throughout the trial, and no one could believe that he had once been an insignificant clerk. He was sentenced to die in the gas chamber, and was duly executed.

BITE OF REVENGE

James McKimmey, Jr.

Erwin—his father would never call him that, it was his late mother's selection—walked slowly across the field away from the old stone quarry, hoisting the chunks of wood he'd gotten from the pile sawed there and not yet stored in the tool shed near the house.

It was midsummer, but the air was raw and chill in this early California morning; and Erwin wished that his father had borrowed the pickup truck from the main house on the ranch and had transferred the wood so that he wouldn't have to carry it a half mile by hand the way he was doing. But his father hadn't and his father would still want a fire when he got up on this Sunday morning.

Thus Erwin, a tall, skinny boy in worn and dirty blue jeans and brown wool jacket, trudged along toward the small, aging frame house, the metal-framed spectacles on his nose steaming over from the exertion.

He moved slowly but steadily, avoiding the reddish tri-leafed growths of poison oak; his fair skin was very susceptible to rash. He also watched the stubble of grass where there might be rattlesnakes. Erwin would be twelve years old next August, but he knew his way around this ranch where his father worked as a hand.

And so had Bolo. Thinking of that, Erwin's throat got tight all over again, and the blurring of his glasses seemed to get worse as his eyes got hot. He'd had Bolo for over four years; they'd been companions day and night.

Erwin passed the pump shed now, listening carefully to the rhythmic grind of the pump inside. He'd repaired the belt yesterday, and it was still holding together. They really needed a new belt, but his father wouldn't buy one. He left it up to Erwin to see that the old one kept working. And when it didn't, there was a cuff on the ear, a blast of cursing . . .

Erwin carried the wood inside and put it by the stove in the large kitchen. The house was very old. It had served as quarters for a long line of ranch hands and their families for some fifty years now. But it had looked very neat when Erwin's mother had been alive. It had been warm and clean and always smelled good from freshly baked bread. Now it was all different, including the smell. It smelled now of cheap wine, even though Erwin had thrown away the empty bottle earlier.

Erwin put old newspapers into the stove, then some kindling, and then the larger wood. He lit the paper just as his father appeared from the bedroom, eyes red-rimmed, a black stubble of beard on his face, still wearing the clothes he'd finished work in, the late afternoon before. The smell of wine became stronger.

"About time," his father said, walking heavily and unsteadily across to the kitchen sink. "You'd get up when you're supposed to, you'd get your chores done on time." His father filled a glass with water from the tap, drank it greedily, then drank another. His father was large, hulking about the shoulders, dark and weather-burned.

"I got up early," Erwin said.

His father drank another glass of water.

"I got up soon's it was light," Erwin said, "so I could bury Bolo."

His father turned around finally, looking at him with disdain and an anger caused unreasonably by the aching of his head, the insatiable thirst. "You're not so prompt," he said, "with chores that need to be done."

Erwin looked down at his hands through his spectacles. "What'd you have to go and kill him for?"

His father frowned, knitting black bushy eyebrows. "Why'd I want to kill that worthless dog? Why wouldn't I—" Then he stopped speaking, eyes shifting a little, and Erwin thought he was remembering how he'd kicked the dog again and again, until . . .

"I still don't know why," Erwin said. "Why—why'd you do it?"

His father stared at him for a moment, then turned and splashed water from the tap into his face. He didn't answer. He wouldn't, Erwin knew. If it was something he didn't like, he just wouldn't talk, ever. It had been like that after his mother had . . .

Erwin compressed his thin lips, the vague shadows of memories returning. His mother had died three years ago, and those memories kept returning: that night, the black voice of his father growing stronger, angrier, while Erwin curled tighter in his bunk on the porch, pulling Bolo close in beside him. They had gone long distances that day, he and Bolo, and fatigue was strong. The black voice turned thunderously mean, and then there had been the scuffling sound; but Erwin had seen his father stumble drunkenly before. He'd slept despite all of that, drifting away.

And then morning had arrived, and there had been his father coming into the house, just at dawn, face gray, eyes red-rimmed. His father had telephoned immediately, without telling Erwin what had happened, and afterward Erwin thought about how happy his mother had been to have that telephone she'd always wanted and pleaded with his father for, and how it was that same telephone that his father used to say that his mother was lying at the foot of the stone quarry, dead.

He'd tried to talk to his father, later, to ask him why his mother would have been up at that time of day walking by the quarry where that slide of crumbled rock had smashed into her and nearly buried her—why, when she almost never went over there. But his father shut him up quickly and would never talk about it.

The men in the uniforms had asked his father the same kind of questions about how Erwin's mother had been over there, but all he would tell them, over and over, was, "I don't know—she was a good woman, a good woman." Erwin wondered how his father could seem to mean that so much when he'd seen his father, with the smell of sweet wine strong from his lips, turn mean with her, ugly . . .

Erwin put those memories out of his head. He straightened his thin shoulders a little.

His father turned around, another glass of water in his hand. "Better check that belt on the pump. I don't want that thing breaking down again. And don't be fooling around with that car, do you hear?"

The pump breaking down and the consequent interruption of the house's water supply had become almost a mania with his father; it was something to build new angers with, to spark new rages. Erwin checked the fire in the stove, pausing just long enough to half close his eyes and remember how it had been once.

There was a bare spot on the small shelf where the telephone had been, and once again Erwin remembered how happy his mother had been when that telephone had been installed. "Four miles from anybody out here, and it makes me feel comfortable, safe . . ."

Now it was gone. His father didn't want to waste any money on it.

"Hurry up," his father said, drinking water again.

Erwin got his pair of old pliers from a pantry drawer, shoved them into his hip pocket, and walked outside.

He didn't go straight to the pump shack, because there was a storm of resentment building inside him that morning. Instead he walked across the dirt drive, past the dusty 1950 sedan, brushing his fingers over the metal of the hood. Erwin liked mechanical things, and when his father wasn't around, he would pull up the hood and check over the engine, loosening and tightening nuts, removing the spark plugs and wiping them clean and replacing them. He would have liked to make his own mechanical things, but he didn't own the materials or any tools, with the exception of a pair of pliers.

He walked on back of the tool shed—it wasn't really a tool shed, it was just called that; all there was in it was a rake and a spade and an old rusty saw—and stopped some forty yards beyond, where he kneeled down beside a mound of fresh earth. He'd put a large stone at the head of that mound, and now he placed his hands gently on the stone and once again his glasses blurred and his eyes got hot.

Bolo hadn't been all beagle, but just a part. But he'd looked mostly like a beagle, even if he was bigger and his nose was too long.

He could run terribly fast, and he had just as good a sense of smell as any hunting dog. Erwin didn't own any kind of gun, but he could have shot all of a thousand rabbits if he had, because that was how many Bolo had tracked down. Mr. Kindler, who owned the ranch and lived in the main house four miles away, had said Bolo was as good a hunting dog as any he'd ever seen. And four times he had taken Bolo out to hunt, and got a rabbit each time.

Erwin's glasses were all steamed now, and tears were streaming hotly down his cheeks. He kept thinking about how Bolo had looked when he was running, kicking out those short, muscular back legs, pumping with them, and as fast as the wind. Now—Erwin wanted to forget how Bolo had whimpered when that first kick had struck him ...

Erwin stood up blindly, not able to see anything for a long time, until he'd finally admitted that he was really crying and got out a dirty handkerchief and wiped his eyes dry and put the spectacles back on.

Then Erwin walked back past the tool shed and toward the pump shack. The pump was silent now, and Erwin hoped it was because enough water had been temporarily pumped into the pipes and not because the belt had broken again. He didn't know if he could fix that belt again or not, it was so worn.

He opened the door of the weather-gray structure that held the pump and looked inside. It was muddy in there from water leaking, and it smelled musty. The belt, Erwin saw, was all right. It was just that enough water was in the pipes ...

And then Erwin saw something else. His eyes widened a little, and he stepped back suddenly, but softly and carefully. He stared inside for a moment; then he turned and ran part way to the house.

Then he stopped. He stopped quickly, a flush of excitement in his face. He stood there through a long pause, frowning a little. His mother had always said that Erwin had a good, quick brain and despite the fact that his father disliked the skinny look of him, she'd always said that you couldn't beat Erwin's quick thinking.

Erwin turned then and walked to the car quickly. He glanced toward the house, then released the hood and got out his pliers. He worked swiftly, then replaced the hood and went to the tool shed, where he got the rake.

He carried the rake to the pump shack, looking back at the house once more, then he looked in the shack. The pump was running once more. Carefully, Erwin turned the rake backwards and extended the handle inside, slowly, until the tip of it touched the switch handle on the wall. He pushed down and the pump stopped.

Erwin stepped back, drawing the handle of the rake out, then he made his way quickly back to the tool shed. There he waited, back from the door in the darkness. He waited, hopefully.

Minutes went by, one by one, and then his father, dark and angry, burst out of the house. "That pump's off again!" his father shouted. "Now get it fixed! Hear me? Get it fixed."

Erwin didn't move. He didn't answer.

His father stood there, eyes blazing, looking around the yard, then he marched to the road and down to the pump shack, muttering angrily. He kicked at the door, stomping inside. Erwin waited, tense. The blood was pounding in his eyes and ears.

A second later, there was a scream, and his father was crashing out, eyes wide in disbelief. His father stood there for a moment, one hand grabbing the calf of his right leg, then he whirled, stumbled and fell, picked himself up, and ran back toward the house, yelling and swearing.

A dozen yards from the house he stopped, turning, throwing his arms out wildly and shouting, "Erwin! Erwin!"

Erwin had never heard his father call him by his name— it was always "kid" or some sort of swear word or nothing at all. Erwin was interested in the way his father was calling him "Erwin" now. But he didn't answer. He didn't move. He waited.

He waited until his father suddenly ran to the car, got in, and ground his foot against the starter.

The starter whirred strongly. It whirred over and over.

But the car didn't start. And his father was screaming once again, face blanched with panic and fear. Erwin was also surprised that his father was reacting this way. He was just wild, and he wasn't even attempting to cut the bite with X's and suck the poison out. All he did was keep that starter whirring over and over, all the time yelling, "Erwin! Erwin!"

Erwin didn't know exactly how long he waited in the shed. He waited quite a long time, however. The starter wasn't whirring anymore when he did step out into the sunshine. And his father wasn't yelling anymore.

It was very quiet when Erwin walked back to the car, reached around the still form of his father and released the hood once again. Erwin was surprised at how quiet it was.

But he was used to solitude. Still, when he'd replaced the spark plugs into the car, locking them tight with his pliers, and started out on the four-mile walk to the main house to tell them about his father and that rattlesnake, he was feeling lonely again. He wished that Bolo was running up ahead of him, those strong, short legs pumping. Erwin's glasses blurred all over again, but still he felt better now. A lot better.

LILY BELL

Richard Deming

Most people thought Lily Bell Winston was about as flighty as they come, but when you got to know her as well as I did, you realized there was a hard core of practicality under her flibbertigibbet exterior. True, she wasn't very constant in her relationships with fellows before she got married, but even as a teenager she knew what she wanted out of life. She would have liked both romance and security in marriage, but when she realized it was a choice of one or the other, she picked the latter.

In a way I couldn't blame her, for she'd never had a thing before marriage. Her widowed ma ran the only boarding-house in Pig Ridge Center, which was hardly a big deal when you consider that the village's population was only three hundred. I guess she figured that trading the poverty of her home life for marriage with either me or Skeeter Hawkins would be jumping from the frying pan into the fire.

Skeeter Hawkins and I courted Lily Bell all through high school. Though nobody, including Lily Bell, I think, could ever really tell which of us she preferred, it was generally accepted throughout Pig Ridge County that eventually she'd pick one or the other. It shocked the whole countryside when, the summer after we all graduated, she up and married somebody else.

She broke the news of her decision to me first, which was some consolation. It led me to believe I might have won out over Skeeter if a third choice hadn't entered the picture.

She came down to the houseboat where Pa and I lived to search me out. Though it was a hot day in mid-July, she looked as cool and fresh in a pink-and-white gingham dress as though it were sixty-five instead of a hundred and two in the shade. Her cornsilk hair was tied into a pony tail by a pink ribbon, making her look about fourteen instead of the nearly nineteen she was. My heart started to thump the moment I spotted her working her way with cat-footed sureness down the steep river bank.

I had just started to run a trot line from the stern of the houseboat to a buoy Pa had set out just this side of the channel. When I saw Lily Bell coming down the bank, I rowed the skiff back to the houseboat, tied it up and was on deck by the time she reached the board we used as a gangplank. I remember wishing I'd had more notice of her visit because I wasn't wearing a thing but a ragged old pair of denims, not even shoes, and the houseboat was in its usual state of messiness.

She skipped up the gangplank, looked around and asked abruptly, "Mr. Harrow here?"

"Pa's up in the village," I said.

She nodded. "I figured he'd be loafing in the tavern on a day like this. I wanted to see you alone."

I gave her a pleased grin.

Then the grin faded when she said, "I'm getting married, Pete."

"Skeeter?" I asked sourly.

She shook her head. "Before I tell you who, I want you to know why. I guess both you and Skeeter deserve that. I'm really quite fond of you both, you know."

"But fonder of somebody else, huh?" I said with a touch of bitterness.

She shook her head again. "I'd marry one of you in a minute, if either of you had any future. But what can either of you offer a wife?"

I felt myself flush. "We're barely out of high school and are just nineteen years old. You can hardly expect us to be millionaires yet."

"You'll never even be hundredaires. I know your ambitions, Pete. You'll spend summers on the river fishing, winters in the hills trapping, just like your pa. Would you expect me to come live on this houseboat and breed a flock of future river rats?"

My flush deepened. "Pa's always got along. He made enough from fishing and trapping to put me through high school, didn't he?"

Her lips formed a pitying smile. "What good's an education you never intend to use?"

"What kind of work you expect me to do? There aren't more than a dozen paying jobs in the village, and they're all filled. If you don't own land in this county, you got to fish and trap."

"There're jobs in the city."

That wasn't fair because she knew I'd never leave Pig Ridge County. Nobody with any sense would. There wasn't a more peaceful, beautiful place in the world. Maybe we were a little backward, but we knew how to enjoy life without rush. Despite her ambitions, Lily Bell wouldn't have thought of moving to the city herself. She had an older sister who had married and moved there, and every time Lily Bell visited her, she came back swearing she'd die before she ever traded Pig Ridge County life for that kind of rat race.

"Would you go with me?" I demanded.

"There's no point in discussing that," she said. "I didn't come here to argue with you. I just wanted to tell you my plans, so there'd be no hard feelings between us."

"You told Skeeter yet?"

"No, but I will. His prospects are about the same as yours. He'll spend twenty years helping his pa work that thirty acres of dirt farm, then when his paw dies, he and his brother will inherit fifteen acres apiece."

I wasn't about to argue Skeeter Hawkins' case. I asked, "Who's the lucky man?"

She took a deep breath before saying, "Bill Skim."

My eyes widened in shock. "That old crab!" I blurted. "Why, he must be forty years old."

"Thirty-eight," she said. "And the richest bachelor in the county. Five hundred acres of clear land, forty milk cows, fifty thousand dollars' worth of paid-for farm machinery, a beautiful big house and ten thousand dollars in the bank."

"It sounds like he rendered you a financial statement along with his proposal," I said caustically.

"He did. I guess he figured he had to offer some concrete inducement to balance his looks. He's hardly as handsome as either you or Skeeter."

"Thanks for nothing," I said. "He's hardly as handsome as the scarecrows he sets out in his fields."

"Don't be bitter, Pete. I want to part friends."

"We'll continue to speak," I growled.

"I mean real friends. I'd like to think that if I ever really needed anything, I could still call on you for help."

She looked at me so wistfully, I couldn't help smiling through my pain. "You know damn well I'd come running whenever you needed me, even ten years from now and if I was married to someone else, which I won't be."

"You'll find another girl," she assured me. "You and Skeeter both. Good-by, Pete."

She flitted toward me, stood on tiptoe to plant a quick kiss on my mouth, then was running back across the gang-plank.

Skeeter Hawkins and I had never been friends, but our mutual misery drew us together on Lily Bell's wedding day. I guess we were about the only two members of our high-school graduating class who didn't attend the wedding. We wandered separately into Juniper Joe's, the only tavern in Pig Ridge Center, and ended up getting drunk together.

It was a mistake because, while we started out sympathizing with each other, by closing time too much whisky had brought out our natural antagonism. Skeeter said something I didn't like—I was too drunk to remember what—and I invited him out back.

By then all the customers but us had gone home. When we staggered out the back door, Juniper Joe locked it behind us from inside, so there was no one to break it up.

Sober we might have killed each other, since we both stood six feet two and weighed in the neighborhood of two hundred pounds. But we were too drunk to hurt each other much. We stumbled around missing each other with roundhouse swings and falling down from our own momentum. We both ruined our clothes and skinned our knees, but I can't remember either of us landing a clean blow.

Finally Skeeter got sick and I had to hold his head. Afterward we shook hands, each of us assuring the other he'd put up a hell of a fight.

The incident didn't convert us into friends, despite our concluding handshake. When we sobered up, we didn't dislike each other any more than before, but we didn't like each other any better either. We just resumed the status quo of staying as much as possible out of each other's way.

I didn't see much of either Lily Bell or Skeeter during the next year. I had a couple of casual encounters with Skeeter, and once I saw Lily driving through the village in a new car, but she must not have seen me because she didn't even wave. I stayed pretty close to the river until it got cold, then spent the whole winter up at our Pig Ridge shack trapping fur. I got into the village only a few times during the whole year.

Pa kept me abreast of the news, though, because summer or winter he never missed a Saturday at Juniper Joe's. And the tavern was the village hub of gossip.

According to Pa, Lily Bell was living in pretty high style for Pig Ridge County. Bill Skim had bought her the new car I had seen her driving, plus a flock of pretty clothes, and she drove all over the county showing herself off. Skim, who had never attended a barn dance in his life, was now dragged to all of them by his new bride. Pa said he was reported to be as taciturn and dour as ever, but at least he now appeared in public. He seldom danced more than the first dance, Pa said, after which he retired to the bar and glowered at his wife enjoying herself the rest of the evening. There was some talk about the way Lily Bell carried on at dances with young unmarried sparks, particularly with Skeeter Hawkins.

Another year passed, with me still staying pretty much to myself. According to Pa, Lily Bell was still flitting all over the county and continuing to be the belle of the ball at barn dances. Then, during the summer, he brought home some news of Skeeter Hawkins.

"Young Skeeter Hawkins got himself a job," he announced.

I hiked my brows and waited.

"Jim Biggs resigned as deputy, and Sheriff Hill put Skeeter on."

I felt a touch of envy. In an essentially farming community such as ours, sheriff's deputy was one of the few salaried jobs of any consequence. And for a young man Skeeter's age, it had a lot of future. Sheriff Albert Hill was past sixty, and none of his other four deputies were much short of forty. In a little over fifteen years they would all be past retirement age and Skeeter would be senior deputy in terms of service. By thirty-five or -six he could very well be county sheriff.

If I had known of the vacancy, I would have applied for the job myself, but I hadn't heard of it.

Along toward the end of August, on a Saturday afternoon, Lily Bell paid a visit to the houseboat. I glanced up from cleaning a channel cat at the sound of a car pulling off on the road shoulder next to the river bank. Lily Bell climbed from the shiny blue car and picked her way daintily down the bank. She was wearing a pink knit suit, nylon stockings and high-heeled shoes.

As usual during hot weather, I was wearing nothing but worn denims. I tossed the catfish into a bucket and wiped my hands on a rag as she came across the gangplank. I noticed that she had a black eye.

"Hello, Pete," she said without smiling. "I was just driving by and decided to drop in. Mr. Harrow around?"

She knew Pa wouldn't be there on a Saturday, so I ignored the question. "What happened to your eye?"

She hesitated a bare second before saying, "I ran into something at the farm."

"Like a fist?" I inquired.

She sat down on the rail, put her face in her hands and began to cry. I had never seen her cry before, and I didn't know what to do. I stood shifting from foot to foot, patting her shoulder and saying, "Please don't cry, Lily Bell. Please don't cry."

After a while she dried her eyes on a tiny handkerchief, sniffed a couple of times and asked in a despairing voice, "What am I going to do, Pete?"

Even with the rage against her husband seething inside me, I couldn't resist an I-told-you-so remark. "It's not working out as wonderful as you thought, huh?"

She looked up at me reproachfully. "I thought you were going to stay my friend, Pete."

"Sorry," I said. "I am your friend. Is this the first time?"

She shook her head. "About the tenth. He's getting worse all the time. I can hardly leave the place any more without there being a scene when I get home. He accuses me of all sorts of things. He seems to have it fixed in his mind that I'm carrying on some kind of affair with Skeeter, for instance, just because I've danced with him a few times at dances."

When I didn't say anything, she said, "I swear I haven't given him any reason for suspicion. I've been a good wife. What am I going to do, Pete?"

"Leave him."

"And go back to living in that awful boardinghouse with Ma?"

What could I say to that? Offer her a bunk in the houseboat? That would be a comedown even from the boardinghouse.

"Well, you can't keep getting beat up," I said. "Why don't you have him arrested?"

She gazed at me from frightened eyes. "You don't know his temper," she whispered. "He'd kill me as soon as he got out of jail."

"He's not going to kill anybody," I told her. "Wait until I get a shirt and shoes on and I'll ride back home with you. I'll convince that so-and-so that if he ever lays a hand on you again, I'll stretch his neck until he looks like a goose."

Jumping up, she said in a terrified voice, "Please don't, Pete. Please don't interfere."

I hiked my eyebrows, "If you don't want me to interfere, why'd you come here?" I asked brusquely.

"For sympathy, I guess. I can see it was a mistake. Please promise you'll forget my visit. Don't mention it to anyone or do anything about it."

"I'm not going to say or do anything you wouldn't want me to," I assured her. "I thought you were asking my help."

"No. I never should have come. Just forget I did." She hurried back across the gangplank before I could say anything more.

I kept my word and never even mentioned her visit to Pa. A couple of weeks later I did casually ask if he'd seen or heard anything of the Skims.

Pa said he'd seen them a few times and they looked fine to him. "Now that you mention it, I hear Lily Bell ain't seen gallivanting around alone so much as she used to," he said. "I also heard the last barn dance they went to, she spent most of the evening sitting on the sidelines next to Bill instead of leaving him at the bar while she danced. Maybe she's starting to settle down."

She had solved her problem by restricting her activities so that her husband had no reason for suspicion, I decided. I hated to think of her cooped up in that big house with no one but dour Bill Skim for companionship, but it had been her choice. I tried to push the matter from my mind.

I hadn't really succeeded when the first snow fell in early November. I had a lot of time to think about Lily Bell because I was up at our Pig Ridge shack all alone by then. Pa had retired from trapping now that I was old enough to handle it myself and didn't have to go to school in the wintertime. He still did his share of setting and clearing the trot lines in the summer because he liked fishing, but he said the cold of winter was beginning to get in his bones.

I had been alone at the shack for two weeks when Lily Bell paid me a visit. Our shack was right beneath the crest of Pig Ridge in the heart of the hills, and the closest you could get to it by road was three miles. After that you had to cross two low hills, then climb nearly to the top of Pig Ridge. At this time of year the only way you could make it was on snowshoes or skis.

I always used both in the hills, skis downhill and snowshoes up, but Lily Bell came up to the shack equipped only with snowshoes and had to tramp the whole way.

She was waiting for me inside the shack when I returned about four P.M. from my daily check of the traps. She was seated on the lower part of the double bunk, wearing ski pants and a blouse. Her fur-lined parka hung from the back of a chair and her snowshoes stood in one corner. Her shiny, cornsilk-colored hair was, as usual, tied into a pony tail by a pink ribbon.

She had the lantern going and a fire burned in the wood stove. I tossed the bag containing two beaver and a fox in a corner, leaned my rifle in the same corner, stripped off my parka and hung it up.

"Aren't you even going to say hello?" she asked.

"I'm trying to recover from my surprise," I said. "I saw your tracks leading to the door, but just figured it was some hunter. Hello."

She gave me a tremulous smile. "Don't you wonder why I'm here?"

I went over to warm my hands at the stove. "Uh-huh. Why are you here?"

"I'm leaving Bill. I can't stand it any more."

I examined her. She didn't show any bruises or contusions. "He still using you as a punching bag?"

She shook her head. "He hasn't hit me since the time I

last saw you. I don't give him any reason. I stay home and we just sit and look at each other. It's driving me crazy. I have to get away from him."

"You're leaving him right now?" I asked. "You're not going back home at all?"

"Oh, yes, I'm going back tonight. For the last time. I'm catching the bus for the city tomorrow afternoon. I'm going to stay with my sister, Abagail, until I decide what to do about a divorce."

I said, "Aren't you going to get banged around if you go home tonight? Where will you say you've been?"

"He isn't home. He had to go to the city for a tractor part, and I don't expect him back until about midnight. I'll be safely in bed by then."

I scratched my chin. "Why'd you come clear up here to tell me all this?"

"Because I need a favor. Once, you told me you'd come running any time I needed you. Does that still hold?"

"Of course. Now, ten years from now, any time."

"When Bill learns I'm leaving him, I'm afraid he'll kill me. As a matter of fact, once when I threatened to, he told me he would if I ever tried it. At the very least, I know there's going to be an awful scene. I want you to come get me about noon tomorrow and drive me to the bus. It leaves at two."

I frowned at her. "Wouldn't it have been simpler to take the bus today while he's gone?"

"You know there was no bus today. It runs only three times a week."

I had known that, but I had lost track of what day it was.

I said, "Why don't you drive up to your sister's tonight? It's only about eighty-five miles."

"Bill took the car. I came here in the pickup truck. I doubt the pickup would hold together for eighty-five miles. It's about ready to fall apart."

"All right," I said. "I'll be along to get you at noon. I'll go down to the houseboat and get the jalopy about eleven. What is tomorrow?"

"Saturday," she said in surprise.

"Then Pa won't be around and I won't have to make any explanation. You better start back now before it gets dark. I'll walk you back to your truck."

"No," she said quickly. "I know these hills as well as you do. I'll be all right."

I told her I preferred to accompany her, but she insisted it would be ridiculous to make the round trip when she was quite capable of getting back to the road by herself.

"I got here all right, didn't I?" she said. "It's mostly downhill on the way back, and I can easily make it by dark. You'd have to make the climb back here all by yourself in the dark."

There was something to that, and I had already spent a full day on snowshoes. Reluctantly I let her talk me into staying behind.

While my supper was cooking, and periodically while I was eating it, I watched from the shack window until she reached the top of the first hill beyond Pig Ridge. It was almost dusk by then, but she had only about three-quarters of a mile more to go and only one more low hill to climb. I knew she would reach the road before dark.

I washed the dishes, skinned the day's catch, and went to bed.

It wasn't nearly the problem getting home from Pig Ridge that it was getting there. I didn't need snowshoes, but I took them along, slung to my back, because I would need them on the return trip.

Pig Ridge was high enough so that, if you were familiar enough with its slopes, you could get up enough momentum on skis to carry you clear to the top of the first hill beyond, over it and three-quarters of the way up the second hill. You had to walk your skis about twenty-five yards to the crest of the second, then it was downhill clear to the road.

It was five miles from there to the houseboat, but it was all on hard-packed snow. There wasn't any traffic because this secondary road was used only by hunters. Not a single car passed in either direction.

As our houseboat was a couple of miles upriver from Pig Ridge Center, I didn't have to pass through the village. When I arrived home about eleven A.M., I had encountered no one at all.

Pa wasn't home, of course. As it was Saturday, he would be at Juniper Joe's. I stowed away my skis, snowshoes and rifle, shed my hunting clothes and took a bath. Then I dressed in a suit, topcoat and galoshes.

My 1929 Ford coupe was kept in an abandoned barn a few yards up the road from the houseboat. After setting so long, it took me about fifteen minutes to get it started. It was twenty to twelve when I headed for the Skim farm, which would get me there just about noon.

The route led back along the river road, the same way I had come, to Howe Junction, then east past the edge of the hills a couple of miles, then back south along a gravel road about a mile to the farm. It would have been a mile and a half shorter to drive through the village on the main road, but for some reason I preferred not to be seen heading for the farm. If I had thought about it, I would have realized I was going to be seen dropping Lily Bell at the bus station anyway, but I wasn't thinking that far ahead. It just seemed wise when going to pick up another man's wife to make my approach surreptitiously. I saw only two other cars en route, both driven by strangers.

A couple of dogs came barking from the barn when I drove up the lane and parked next to the big house's side entrance. When I climbed out, they sniffed at my galoshes, wagged their tails and returned to the barn to get out of the cold.

By my watch it was just noon when I knocked at the side door.

About a minute passed before Bill Skim opened the door. He was a lean, narrow-faced man with sunken eyes and a hooked beak over a gash of a mouth. He had thick, jet-black hair as straight as an Indian's, and wore a constantly sullen expression. He was dressed in a flannel shirt and clean overalls.

He gazed at me with no sign of welcome. "What you want, Harrow?"

"Lily Bell. She ready?"

"Lily Bell? What you mean, Lily Bell?"

"Your wife," I said patiently. "I'm driving her into the village."

A scowl grew on his face. "She ain't here. She's in the city visiting her sister."

He started to close the door, but I caught it against my shoulder and bulled my way inside. He fell back and glared at me.

I pushed the door shut behind me and leaned my back against it. "Where is she?" I asked.

"I told you, in the city. What you think you're doing, forcing your way into my house?"

"When did she leave?"

"I druv her in yesterday morning."

I looked at him steadily until he flushed. "What's the matter with you?" he inquired.

"She wasn't in the city yesterday. I saw her at four o'clock."

"You must be crazy," he said. "I dropped her at Abagail's at eleven A.M. What business is it of yours, anyway?"

I said, "I think I'll take a look around."

"You'll get out of here or I'll call the sheriff," he threatened.

I walked over to within six inches of him and gazed down into his face. He was a head shorter than me and a good sixty pounds lighter. He backed away nervously.

"I'm going to look through the house," I informed him. "You're going to tail along and keep your mouth shut. Give me a hard time and I'll tie you in a fisherman's knot."

He gazed at me as though he suspected I was crazy. Licking his lips, he said, "I don't want no trouble with you, Harrow. Do your looking, then get out."

There was no sign of Lily Bell in any of the downstairs rooms. I had Skim precede me up the stairs to the second floor. There were four rooms and a bath up there. Two of the rooms were fitted out as bedrooms, one was used for storage, and the fourth was locked.

When I had checked the three unlocked rooms and the bath without finding Lily Bell, I held out my hand.

"Get up the key to this room."

"That's Lily Bell's sewing room," he said. "She must have the key. I didn't even know it was locked."

I was in no mood to argue. I hit the door with my shoulder and broke the lock.

"Hey!" Skim squawked.

Then he fell silent as he moved into the room behind me and saw what I was looking at. In the center of the carpet was a huge round spot of clotted blood. There was a splash of it on the sewing machine and several smaller splashes on one wall.

I felt a throbbing start in my head. I turned toward Skim, whose jaw was hanging slackly open. At the expression on my face he backed into the hall, inching out.

"Cut yourself shaving?" I asked, moving toward him.

He held both hands protectively before him. "Now wait a minute, Harrow. You got no call—"

I shut him off by gathering a fistful of shirt and shaking him until his teeth rattled. When I released him, he stumbled across the corridor into the far wall.

"I guess there's no point in asking you about it," I growled at him. "We'll do some more looking."

I pushed him ahead of me toward the stairs. He went down them throwing cringing looks back over his shoulder at me, as though afraid I might belt him from behind at any moment.

This time I made a more thorough search of the down-stairs. The first time I had only looked in places big enough to conceal a woman or her body. This time I peered into everything.

There was a combination summer kitchen and laundry room off the regular kitchen. It had set tubs in it, a washing machine, and an old-fashioned wood and coal range. When I lifted one of the cast-iron lids on top of the range, I saw charred cloth inside.

I pulled out a half-burned dress. What was left of it was covered with dried blood.

Probing further, I drew out several articles of women's underclothes, similarly charred and bloodstained, a pair of women's shoes, and a pink hair ribbon which was literally soaked with blood.

Bill Skim stared at the pile of clothing glassily, seemingly incapable of speech.

I pushed him ahead of me toward the door of the wood-shed giving off the summer kitchen. In a half-empty wood box there was a bloodstained axe with several strands of long, cornsilk-colored hair clinging to it.

By now my head was throbbing steadily. With effort I restrained myself from picking up the axe and burying it in Skim's skull.

"Better get a jacket and boots on," I said quietly. "We're going outside."

"Listen," he said. "I don't know what this is all about."

Barely moving my lips, I said, "If you so much as open your mouth again, I'll kill you. Get on your wraps."

He didn't give me any more argument. He was so scared, he practically flew to get dressed for outdoors.

I found what I was looking for behind the barn. Snow had been cleared from an area about six feet by three and there was a mound of fresh-turned dirt in the cleared space, clinching all my suspicions.

After both of us had gazed at it for a time, I said dully, "What time did you get back from the city yesterday?"

"What?" he asked, gazing at me stupidly.

"What time did you get back from the city yesterday?" I rasped at him. "Get up an answer fast."

He backed a step away from me and whispered, "About five in the afternoon. Why?"

So he had been home when Lily Bell returned from her visit to me, I thought. I wondered if she had made the mistake of admitting where she had been and that she planned to leave him today.

It didn't really matter what had brought it about. All I could think of was that I would never see Lily Bell again. The throbbing in my head became unbearable. I don't even remember reaching for his throat. But when I finally released it, he wasn't struggling any more.

I left him lying next to the grave and plowed my way back to the car. When I started the engine, the dogs came barking from the barn again. They followed the car down the lane to the road, barking it on its way, then trotted back toward the barn with wagging tails.

I took the same route back to the houseboat that I had used to get to the farm. It wasn't by plan because my mind was a total blank. It was pure instinct that kept me from driving through the village, where I couldn't have avoided being seen by a dozen or more people.

I was back at the houseboat before it really registered on me that I had committed murder. Then it occurred to me that no one at all knew I had come down from the hills.

I parked the car in the abandoned barn, changed back into my hunting clothes and hung my good clothes up. Slinging my skis over my back, I picked up my rifle in one hand, my snowshoes in the other, and glanced around to see if I had left any evidence of my visit. I couldn't detect any.

Outside I strapped on my snowshoes because I wasn't going to use the road. Instead I followed the river edge, below the bank and out of sight of the road. Beyond Howe

Junction I finally cut across the road and crossed a couple of open fields to the edge of the hills.

It was just turning dusk when I reached the shack. I hadn't seen a single person all the way back.

It snowed that night, so that even my tracks were covered.

I stayed up on Pig Ridge a full two weeks, then packed up my furs and brought them down the first week in December. It was a Friday afternoon when I arrived at the houseboat, so Pa was home, alone.

It was some time before we got around to conversation. First Pa had to examine all the pelts and figure out what they would bring. Then I had to clean up and change clothes. But eventually we were settled over a couple of cups of coffee in the galley.

"Any gossip while I was up on Pig Ridge?" I asked.

"Yeah, Bill Skim got himself killed by some transient. Strangled, he was. Skeeter Hawkins was assigned the case, but he ain't caught the feller who done it yet."

"Oh?" I said, and waited for him to tell me of the discovery of Lily Bell's grave.

"Lily Bell was in the city visiting her sister Abagail," Pa went on. "Bill had been dead a couple of days when she got back and found him. Stock was in a bad way. Hadn't been fed for forty-eight hours and the cows hadn't been milked. You'd have thought their bawling would have attracted somebody's attention, but nobody heard 'em."

A dizziness passed over me. Just in time I avoided blurting out, "Lily Bell's still alive?"

I burned my throat draining my coffee cup and rose to my feet. As I started to pull on my galoshes, Pa asked, "Where you going?"

"Out," I said shortly.

All the way to the Skim farm my mind was racing. I had it pretty well figured out by the time I reached the farm, so I wasn't very surprised when Skeeter Hawkins answered the door. He looked quite handsome in his gray deputy sheriff's uniform.

"Come on in," he said cordially. "We've kind of been expecting you to show up eventually."

Lily Bell was seated in the front room with a teacup in her lap. There was another on the low table before the sofa.

"Hello, Pete," she said with a smile. "Skeeter just dropped in, and now you. Have a cup of tea?"

"No, thanks," I said politely. "I just dropped by to make sure you're not dead."

"Why would you think that?" she asked, her smile turning to a frown.

"Don't play games with me," I said. "You played me for a chump, but you don't have to rub it in."

"What are you talking about?"

I said, "That Friday you showed at the shack, Bill had driven you into the city to your sister's. You must have furnished Skeeter a key to the house so that he could set the scene while both you and your husband were away. He did a beautiful job. The clues were hidden just enough to make it convincing, but not so thoroughly that I couldn't find them without much trouble. The hairs clinging to the axe is the touch I like best. It was actually your hair, I suppose, but it sure as hell wasn't your blood. What was it? Chicken blood?"

Skeeter said, "Do you know what he's talking about, honey?"

"Shut up," I told him. "Skeeter drove into the city after he'd set the scene here, picked you up and brought you back to the edge of the hills. The reason you didn't want me to accompany you back to the road wasn't because it would inconvenience me. It was because you didn't want me to know you had lied about coming in the pickup truck. Skeeter was waiting for you in his car. He drove you back to your sister's and nobody could prove you'd ever left the city. The next afternoon Skeeter came out here after I'd left and cleaned up all evidence of your 'murder.' You waited a couple of days to assure your alibi, then came back and discovered Bill dead. Did he ever really beat you?"

She smiled at me. "Not really. He wasn't a violent man. Just dull. I blacked my own eye."

Skeeter said, "Bill was strangled by some unknown transient, Pete. You're not suggesting it was anything else, are you?"

After staring at him for a time, I turned around and walked out of the house.

Skeeter and Lily Bell were married six months after Bill Skim's funeral. He resigned his deputy job to run the farm.

Lily Bell now has everything she ever wanted, security and a man she can love.

The thing that grates on me most is that the two of them couldn't possibly have known in advance that I'd get down to the farm, then back into the hills without ever being seen by anyone. They must have expected me to get caught and be hanged. Skeeter was kind enough to cover for me when it turned out I was never suspected, but even that couldn't have been from the goodness of his heart. It simply would have complicated things for him and Lily Bell if I had told my story. And I can't tell anybody what really happened without putting my own neck in a noose.

FLORA AND HER FAUNA

C. B. Gilford

"He'll have to be killed today."

Flora uttered the sentence in mournful tone. Her fat body, wrapped in the faded old kimono, trembled with an accumulation of sorrow. Her tear-stained face, the color and texture of dough, was a mask of desolation.

"Poor Rani. Oh, Howard, I shall have to kill him."

He stared at her. "*You* kill him, Flora!"

"Do you think I could let anybody else do it?"

He blinked. "I don't know. I didn't think you had it in you, Flora. Killing, I mean."

"But Rani is in pain, Howard, so it won't be murder, but mercy killing."

"Sure, mercy killing." He looked at her. Her hands were trembling violently. "Better let me do it, Flora."

"No!" She took a step toward him, enraged, and he fell back, afraid of her, as always.

Yes, he was afraid of her. He had to admit it in moments like this. He was afraid of a woman, of his own wife, but he always had been. No excuse; there it was—afraid.

"All right, Flora. I was just trying to be helpful."

"Don't you dare touch Rani! Don't come near him!"

"All right, I won't."

He wouldn't touch Rani because he was afraid of her. He hated Rani, hated him with a cold passion, as he hated all of Flora's creatures; and Flora, too; fear and hate.

"How will you kill him, Flora?" He couldn't help feeling curiosity, too.

"I have the poison already."

"You have poison?"

She reached into the pocket of her stained, tattered sweater, and drew out a small bottle. It was filled with a colorless liquid.

"Mr. Grotweiler gave me this, on prescription from Dr.

Mason. It doesn't have any taste, or any odor. It works almost instantly, and with very little pain. Just a drop will do the job."

"But you have a whole bottleful."

"For emergencies."

It may have started in his mind then—the idea, the first glimmer, when he saw how easily it could be done. It was just a notion, vague, unformed, but growing.

"I'll just mix it with some of Rani's food," Flora was saying, "and he'll never know the difference."

Horror on her face, Flora stopped suddenly and put her hand over her mouth. "Oh, do you think Rani heard me? I don't want him to know. It would be so much easier for him if he didn't know ahead of time."

Her pale blue eyes rolled as she cast a glance sideways toward Rani. The huge gray tomcat lay stretched on the center cushion of the red velvet sofa. Gray cat hairs cast a gray film over most of the red velvet. The sofa belonged to Rani, and Rani alone. The cat's eyes were half closed. It was doubtful whether he had heard Flora.

"Poor thing. Look at him. So brave. He doesn't complain at all."

No, the beast wasn't complaining. He was sick, probably on his last legs, Howard had to admit. Usually he was stalking through the house, lording it over everybody, so he must be sick. Good riddance.

"Go on now, Howard. I want to be alone with Rani during his last moments."

He left the parlor, closing the double doors behind him with a gentle click. He stood then for a moment, trying to think.

A whir of wings startled him, and a green and yellow meteor flashed past his face. "Stop that!" he shouted between his teeth, softly enough not to be heard by Flora. "You miserable bag of feathers!"

Pericles, the parrot, was perched on a lamp shade, viewing him mockingly. The dive-bombing routine was one of his favorites, because, even though it had been done a thousand times, it never failed to surprise Howard and set him trembling. Now the parrot sat there arrogantly, aware that his victim could exact no vengeance.

"I could kill you!"

No, he couldn't. It was an idle, empty threat. If he could

have killed Pericles, he would have done it long ago. He would have killed them all, every last creature in this ridiculous menagerie!

He had to get out. The heavy stench of animal odors, accumulated over the years, threatened to choke him. There was a layer of moulted fur and feathers over everything, turning into dust, and thence permeating the air. But worst of all were the Presences, the constant Presences, staring at him, watching him.

Along the wall were the aquaria. The inhabitants had stopped their lazy, aimless swimming about, and they were staring at him, too, with their stupid fish eyes. From cages in front of every window, the beady eyes of winged creatures considered him. For the moment they had ceased their chattering just to look at him, the helpless Enemy, as if he were in a cage, not they. They knew he couldn't come near them. Flora wouldn't let him.

As for the creatures who roamed free, they sat on their haunches and stared, too—the cats and the dogs; Fritzie, the noisy little dachshund; Pickles, the nasty-tempered terrier; and worst of all, the disgusting Pekingese, Fan-Tan.

"I hate you!" he flung at them as he headed for the front door.

It was Fan-Tan, as usual, who translated emotion into deeds. Howard heard the scurry of tiny paws behind him. Ignominiously he ran, but not quickly enough. The little red-brown canine overtook him, leaped at his flying ankle, and sank her needle teeth into the retreating flesh.

Howard knew better than to yell. He dragged the dog a few steps, managed to shake her off, and then to put the screen door between them. He ran across the sagging veranda, down the steps, through the weedy yard, and didn't stop for breath until he reached his hideout, the run-down building which had been the stable in the plantation's better days.

Animals had evicted the man from his house. Now the man inhabited the abode of animals.

Howard drank rum from a bottle he kept secreted in the stable, and pondered his present predicament.

Why had he married Flora? Or had Flora merely married him? He must have said yes sometime during the ceremony, but what had he said yes to?

He hadn't been much of a catch, and plenty of women,

before Flora came along, had declined to catch him. He'd been a veterinarian's helper, interested in animals, you might say. That, of course, has given him and Flora "something in common."

So he'd married her. He was dirt poor, and she was sort of rich, in a small way. She owned this piece of land she called a "plantation," with the big old house on it, and had money and bonds and things left her by her daddy, enough to keep it all for safety's sake in several different banks in several different towns.

"You and me," Flora had said, "we'll have a fine life together. You can help me take care of my pets."

He saw her collection of pets, and . . . well, it wouldn't be much different from the kind of things he'd already been doing. The only trouble was, he really didn't *like* animals. He hadn't been exactly a great success as a vet's helper. It had been a job. A ditch-digger doesn't have to *like* the ditches he digs.

So he'd married her, legally anyway. Actually she'd stayed married to her zoo. Howard was simply installed as full-time helper and assistant; same job, new employer.

Only this was much worse: *full-time*. Now he ate, slept, lived with the animals. And most horrible, he was asked to love them.

He cursed softly to himself and swigged his rum. He'd moved into Flora's house because he didn't have one. He hadn't liked the looks of it, but he thought maybe he could clean it up a bit, and maybe, gradually, get rid of at least some of the creatures. No such luck. Flora only added to, never subtracted from her collection. Even the little boy who'd been sent a baby alligator from Florida, and whose mother wouldn't let him keep it, had brought the thing to the one place where he knew it wouldn't be refused. So now an alligator named Alice lived in the bathtub upstairs, the only bathtub in the house. If anyone wanted to take a bath, he first had to remove, then to replace, a two-and-a-half-foot reptile. Usually Howard preferred to go sweaty.

As for meals, they were "family" affairs, as Flora described them. She always had a cat, Rani if he was in the mood, in her lap, eating off her plate whatever tidbits struck the feline fancy. The dog hung around, haughtily demanding. Conversation was, of course, impossible with their constant yapping. Fan-Tan perversely gave her attentions to him. She would nip at his ankles if he would ignore her too long, and then, when he stooped to feed her a morsel, he'd have to withdraw his fingers quickly or she'd have them, too.

"She's your little doggie, Howard," Flora would say, pouting jealously.

The caged beasts weren't quite as bad, except that Howard had to clean their cages, a nasty job. Flora was always too busy. Maybe she'd married him just to get somebody to do that.

Perhaps the crowning indignity, however, had been that perpetrated by Rani. Howard liked his rum. It made life barely endurable. But Rani, attracted by the smell of the hidden bottle, formed a liking for it, too. Flora's first reaction was to decree that the stuff be kept out of the house. Then when Rani meowed inconsolably, she relented. Howard was allowed to keep his rum if Rani could have an eyedropperful once in a while. Rani proved an inveterate guzzler though. He'd seek out the bottle, lick the neck and the cork till it made Howard sick, and sometimes he'd go for days without a drink before he'd touch that unsanitary bottle. Maybe, he thought now with some satisfaction, Rani's fatal illness was alcoholism.

Why hadn't he left it long ago? He'd asked himself that question a million times, and now he asked it again. Why did he put up with it?

Hope? It must be. Hope, and then sheer perseverance. He wouldn't admit defeat by a bunch of animals. He wouldn't let them cheat him out of his inheritance. And he meant to inherit, because Flora was twenty years older than he was, and sooner or later she was going to catch something from all those germs from those unsanitary plates, and then he'd be rich! *Then!* Why not now?

Howard took another swig of rum, and thought of that other bottle which Flora had shown him. No taste . . . no odor . . . works almost instantly . . . just a drop will do the job . . . and there was a whole bottleful.

Flora's piercing scream brought him back to the house on the run. She was standing on the veranda, flailing about with her arms and still screaming, when he arrived.

"He's dead!" she wailed. "Rani is dead!"

"Well, that's what you wanted to accomplish, wasn't it?"

But she wouldn't be comforted by such simple logic. "He didn't want to die. He knew what I was trying to do, but he didn't understand. He didn't even seem to trust me. Then, finally, when he realized what I'd done to him, he looked at me with such reproachful eyes. Oh, Howard, I'll never forget that look. I tried to explain, but he kept shaking his head. Howard, he died thinking I betrayed him."

"Well, we can't have that, can we, Flora?"

"Animals are so wise, Howard. They know who their friends are. But mercy-killing was a little too much for Rani to understand."

"Then you mustn't do it any more, Flora. I mean, you mustn't do it yourself. I should be the one. The animals don't feel the same toward me anyway, so it won't be such a shock to them."

She stared at him through reddened rims. "Maybe you're right."

"Of course I'm right, Flora dear. Just give me the bottle, and when the next time comes, why I'll . . ."

She entrusted him with the bottle, and he hid it in the stable. Afterwards he used a couple of fresh boards to make a little coffin for Rani. He did the work cheerfully, and when he brought the result to Flora, she thought it was beautiful.

Then he took a spade out to the cemetery, which was between the neglected orchard and the old grape arbor. The cemetery was, in fact, the only neatly maintained plot on the whole plantation. Flora had decreed that it be kept fertilized, weeded, and mowed. To Howard's knowledge there were two canaries, several mice—Rani himself had dispatched more than one of them—and a monkey already there. Howard dug a rectangular grave about three feet deep, then informed Flora.

She tried to induce some of the other animals to attend the funeral, but Rani had not been a universally liked member of the community. Pericles and Fan-Tan never left the house, and they made no exception for this event. Pickles, the terrier, attended out of his natural curiosity concerning carrion. Flora carried two of the white mice with her, as a kind of corsage. Howard thought for a while she might have intended to bury the rodents with the coffin, thus giving Rani something of a pharaoh's funeral.

But if she had so intended, she relented at the last moment, and the mice were spared.

It was an impressive ceremony nevertheless. Howard bore the coffin, placed it in the ground, and shoveled the dirt back on top of it. This was the occasion for Flora to burst into hysterical tears, throw herself on the ground, and try to claw the dirt away again. Finally she contented herself with racing madly through the adjoining fields and returning with an armful of wild flowers to strew over the grave. It was sundown before the weeping subsided and Flora allowed herself to be led back into the house.

"One must go on living," she told Howard.

It isn't absolutely necessary, Flora, he answered silently. Not if life is so painful. That's what the stuff in the bottle is for, didn't you say? To kill pain. Should I do any less for you than for Rani, Flora?

"It's supper time," he announced hopefully.

"Oh, I couldn't eat a thing," Flora said hoarsely.

"You've got to keep up your strength, my dear." She was strong as an ox, with plenty of excess fat besides, but he said it anyway. "You have your other responsibilities, remember. To the other animals, I mean. You can't afford to neglect them. Rani wouldn't want you to do that, I'm sure."

She looked at him, her eyes red and bulging, brimming with tears. "I have a big lump in my throat, Howard. I just couldn't swallow."

He had to accept defeat for the moment, but he knew he couldn't delay too long. Proper timing was essential to the motivation he wanted to establish.

Flora was inconsolable. Watching her mope around the house, the animals moped, too. The chattering in the cages stopped. Fan-Tan ceased her yapping, curled on a pillow, and gazed at Flora with unblinking eyes. Pericles sat on his perch without saying a word. A blessed silence reigned, and Howard couldn't help thinking they should have funerals more often around this place.

Flora went to bed without breaking her fast. For hours she tossed and turned, then finally slept. It was late in the morning before she awakened.

"Let me bring you something, Flora," was the first thing he said to her.

"A couple of aspirin," she told him.

"With some orange juice? Would you like some orange juice, Flora?"

"I'll try to down it."

He hurried to the kitchen, opened a can of juice, poured it into a glass over an ice cube. Then he added a stiff shot of the liquid from Mr. Grotweiler's bottle, and stirred. He couldn't tell about the taste, of course, but the concoction smelled of nothing but orange juice. As for the advertised qualities of the stuff, he'd just have to trust Mr. Grotweiler. He wiped his fingerprints from the glass, wrapped a paper napkin around it, and carried it up to Flora.

"You're a dear sweet man, Howard," she said, and these were her last words.

She drank the orange juice thirstily, obviously relishing the taste and unaware of any foreign substance. Afterwards she lay back on the pillow, smiling serenely. This state obtained for perhaps a minute or less. Then a mild frown crossed her face. She looked puzzled, glanced at Howard questioningly, and peacefully closed her eyes.

"Goodbye, Flora," he said.

She didn't answer.

He wasted no time whatsoever after that. It was feeding time at the zoo. Mr. Grotweiler's magic elixir had to be mixed with dog food, cat food, mouse food, rat food, hamster food, fish food and parrot food. He did it all with skill and dispatch.

"Eat heartily, my pets," he crowed as he distributed the treated tidbits.

In the bathroom Alice, the alligator, chewed on a piece of dosed beefsteak, while in the front parlor the fish leaped to the surface of the water to nibble at their little white flakes. For good measure, Howard poured some of the poison straight into the water, too. The rodents positively fought over their morsels, and Howard had to referee to make certain everybody got some. The cats devoured theirs daintily and haughtily. Fritzie and Pickles gave no trouble. Fan-Tan was morose and reluctant, wondering why Flora didn't get out of bed to do the honors, but eventually sheer hunger triumphed. Pericles cocked one eye suspiciously at his poison-soaked seed, but he didn't prove to be nearly as wise as Flora had always thought he was. He pecked at his victuals a few times, and a few pecks were enough.

Howard watched. He wanted to make sure everybody was taken care of. Everybody was.

The fish began floating to the surface. The rodents squeaked shrilly, ran about their cages, and one by one dropped over. The cats meowed a few times, arched their backs, and collapsed. Fritzie barked, Pickles growled, and Fan-Tan yelped for the last time, then lay down and was still. Pericles was the toughest of the lot. He wobbled on his perch, considered the carnage with a cynical gaze, closed one eye, then the other, lost his balance, and fell forward. His claws held onto the round perch, however, so that he hung upside down, swinging gently like a slow pendulum. It was more than a minute before he let go, and the body fell to the floor with a feather-muffled thud.

Howard checked the bathroom. Alice was floating in the tub belly up. He was alone in the house.

Sheriff Crandall was noticeably sympathetic but also profoundly confused as he gazed about at the scene of death and tranquility. "My, my," was all he could say for awhile. "My, my . . ."

"They're all gone," Howard said tearfully. "Every little teeny-weeny fish in the bowls, every little bundle of fur in the cages. And Flora . . ."

"You say she had this bottle full of poison?"

"It only takes a drop, you know, Sheriff, to still those little animal hearts."

"Now it started, you say, with the cat?"

"Right, Sheriff. Rani was her favorite, of course. I'll show you the fresh grave if you like, or dig up the coffin."

"No, no, that won't be necessary, Howard."

"Well, she just couldn't seem to snap out of it. She threw herself on Rani's grave, put flowers on it. You know how Flora was about animals."

"Yes, I guess everybody around here knew about that."

"I finally dragged her back into the house, but there wasn't anything I could say or do to cheer her up. I should have suspected something, I guess."

"Now don't go blaming yourself, Howard. This was just one of those things."

"Well, you know how Flora considered the animals to be her family, and she always wanted to keep the family together. I guess she just went crazy with grief. First poisoned all the animals. Then finally herself. So as to keep the family together."

Sheriff Crandall peered out from under his grizzly brows and scratched his head. "How come she didn't take you along with the rest of 'em, Howard?"

Howard shook his head. "I don't know, Sheriff. I guess it just goes to show where I stood with Flora. She and her pets were sort of blood relatives, and I was just related by marriage."

"I know how you feel, Howard. Sometimes a husband just gets left out in the cold."

They walked out onto the veranda together. It was a nice day, beginning to warm.

"Sheriff," Howard asked, "do you want the bodies for an autopsy, or can I just phone the mortuary?"

"Oh, I don't reckon there's any good reason for an autopsy."

"Well then, there's this other thing. Everybody knows Flora had it in her will. She always wanted to be buried here on the property, in our own private little cemetery."

"Far as I know, Howard, there's no law agin' it."

"And the animals belong there too."

"No law agin' that either."

Sheriff Crandall, glad to be gone, drove away in his dusty pickup. He hadn't been any trouble, none at all.

Howard phoned Mr. Murdock, the undertaker, and gave instructions. Plain, simple coffin for Flora, and he'd take care of the animals himself. No cemetery plot needed. He could save money that way. That was important. It was his money now.

He felt like celebrating. There was that bottle of rum he kept behind the books in the back parlor. He took the bottle to the kitchen and poured himself a glass.

It wasn't until a couple of swallows had gone all the way down his gullet that he began to have the odd sensation—a feeling of dizziness, lightness, fuzziness, a gray fog creeping over him.

Then into the fog came a blinding flash of comprehension. Rani had known what Flora was trying to do to him, to poison him. He had refused the food, the milk, till Flora tricked him with his fatal weakness for rum . . . left it nearby where he could steal a lick of the cork and the wet bottle neck . . . but she'd poisoned the whole bottle!

"Poor old Howard," Sheriff Crandall said. "That last talk we had together. He felt left out. Flora had gone and left him. The animals were all gone. He was all alone. Just couldn't stand the loneliness, I guess. So he just followed along after the rest of the family."

"I understand," said Mr. Murdock the undertaker.

"So I guess we'd better bury 'em all here together in their own private little cemetery."

"Of course," said Mr. Murdock.

"Oh, Howard, you dear sweet man," Flora said, "we've missed you so, even though it wasn't for very long."

A green and yellow meteor flashed before his face and the flutter of parrot wings sent a shudder all through him. He heard a splash of water in the bathtub that could have been made only by an alligator's tail. Fish eyes stared at him from huge glass tanks. Dozens of rodents chattered their welcome. Cats stalked by. A dachshund and a terrier growled fiercely in his direction, and a small Pekingese sank savage, needle-like teeth into his ankle. And there was Rani, the lordly tom, licking the neck and cork of his rum bottle, and smiling with inebriated contempt.

Howard screamed and turned to run, but there was no door. He screamed louder. He knew there were people outside, but his scream was drowned by the din of the earth entombing him.

THE PULQUE VENDOR

Hal Ellson

The great bronze bell in the old Cathedral was tolling the hour. Luis Mendoza, the pulque-vendor, lifted his head, counted eleven strokes and felt the stillness move in on the deserted plaza. Time for the deadly appointment.

He arose from the bench, half-expecting to feel the wooden yoke on his neck and the weight of the two huge jars of pulque which he carried through the streets of the city from sun-up till the hungry shadows of night struck from the desert. Across the plaza he moved, striding rapidly through the shadows cast by sour-orange trees heavy with fruit, past the fountain, then directly across the gutter toward the Municipal Building, dark and mute in its crumbling splendor. A half-dozen police motorcycles stood at the curb in front of Police Headquarters. Inside, a ragged beggar stood bare-headed at a desk, pleading with the officer on duty. Another beggar lay curled on a bench behind the wooden bars of a tiny cell. Mendoza frowned and moved on, rounding the corner into a narrow street, where the shadows swallowed him. He emerged on a large plaza, more desolate than its counterpart, crossed it and vanished into another narrow street much like the one where he lived. Its houses were crumbling and silent, windows dark and barred, with not a single light to indicate the existence of tenants.

Halfway down the street, he stopped abruptly and glanced back. The walk was shadowed and empty. No one had tracked him, and none but the three inside the house where he stood knew of the meeting. For the moment he hesitated, wondering if he could go through with the task. The odds were against him. Others had failed dismally and lay in their graves, shot down by the General's gunmen.

Suddenly he made up his mind and entered the house. Three men awaited him in a small patio barely lit by the pale yellow light of an oil lamp. Greetings were exchanged. Mendoza remained standing and looked from one to the other of the three men. One was old, with white hair and a pale gaunt face. The other two were younger, dark like himself, with the same soft eyes that belied the anger smoldering in them.

The old man was Don Gonzalo Aponte, professor without students, aristocrat without funds. Indirectly, General Macia had deprived him of his post at the university, relieved him of the family hacienda, a proud but crumbling ruin, and appropriated the land surrounding it. The order had been signed by the Governor, who was no more than a puppet. The intent of the General was clear, to break the spirit of Don Gonzalo Aponte.

Aponte's spirit was far from broken, but he was old and weak. To strike back on his own was impossible. Still, there were others who hated the General. Some had been brave enough to join with Aponte, an even dozen men— and nine were already dead, slaughtered by the General's gunmen in three bungled attempts at assassination. Bandits, the newspapers called them, perverting the truth at the request of the General.

Thinking of the dead who'd been buried in the desert where they'd been shot, Aponte nodded to Mendoza. "So you came," he said, measuring the wiry frame of the pulque-vendor.

"I said I'd be here," Mendoza replied with a shrug.

Aponte nodded to the young man on his right. "Your friend, Estaban, recommended you. You know the risk?"

"I know it well."

"Nine men have already died."

"They were unfortunate."

"Death is always unfortunate. If you wish to with-draw . . ."

"I wish no such thing."

A faint smile lit the old man's face. "There are few, if any, who would say that, but a question. Why are you willing to risk so much?"

"Because I am poor, Señor. I have use for the money."

"Many are poor, but . . ."

"Perhaps they like being miserable."

"Then your only concern is the money?"

Mendoza frowned, then shook his head. "The General is

evil, the gunmen are animals. One kills them without feeling. Especially Pancho Negron, who murdered my friend. He has to die."

Aponte nodded and clasped his hands. A diamond ring flashed light. "You are ready?"

"Yes, Señor."

"Then it is tomorrow. You know the Mayor's residence?"

"I know it."

"At noon three cars will be there, and the gunmen. The center car will be for the General. The gunmen will be guarding the street. One will escort the General from the Mayor's residence to the car. A dozen men, all armed." A dry hacking cough wracked the old man. With his fist against his lips, he stemmed the attack and looked at Mendoza. "A dozen men," he repeated.

"I understand," said Mendoza.

"You will have no help. The odds are completely against you."

"It's a gamble," Mendoza conceded. "Twelve against one, but I still possess an advantage."

Aponte failed to see it and asked to be enlightened.

"It's very simple. I am only one man, a poor pulque-vendor," Mendoza explained. "The gunmen will hardly expect trouble from me, and so the element of surprise will be on my side. Besides, I have a plan."

"Which is?"

Mendoza smiled faintly. "That is something I prefer to keep to myself. If it succeeds, or doesn't, you will know about it tomorrow."

Aponte looked at the two younger men beside him and shrugged. "As you wish," he said, turning back to Mendoza.

"And now about the payment?" said the pulque-vendor.

"I see you haven't forgotten that."

"Nor my family," replied Mendoza. "I am doing this for them."

Aponte nodded gravely. "Tomorrow morning at the Cantina of the Matadors you will have your money. As for your mission, I wish you the best of luck."

"I'll need more than that," Mendoza shrugged. "Say a prayer for me." With that, he turned on his heels and left.

As the door closed after him, Aponte shook his head. "A brave fellow, a fool, or . . ."

"Or what?" said Estaban.

"Perhaps he is one of them."

"No, he's all right."

"Perhaps, but if it's money he wants, he may go to the General. It would be worth his while to betray us."

"I've vouched for him. He won't betray us."

Aponte nodded. "Perhaps not. Tomorrow will tell, but I wonder about his plan."

"Whatever it is, it's a gamble. He may kill the General, but he won't survive the gunmen."

"Perhaps he wishes to die."

"No," said Estaban. "But he's poor, and the poor are always desperate."

"He appeared very calm," said Aponte, rising slowly from his chair. His thin face was gaunt with fatigue, his hands had begun to tremble. The two younger men noticed and prepared to leave. As they said good-night and moved toward the door, Aponte halted them. "About the payment," he said to Estaban. "I suggest you leave the money with the barman, properly packaged, just in case. . . ."

"I trust Mendoza. I will give it to him myself," said Estaban.

It was still early, the city awake, clamorous and vibrating with life after the black stillness of sleep. As the bronze bell in the Cathedral crashed out the hour, Mendoza crossed the plaza and stopped before the huge main door with its carved figures worm-eaten and scarred by dry-rot to a point of semi-obliteration. A step brought him beyond the door into the dim interior. At first it appeared empty, but a black-shawled figure knelt on the floor; a sibilant whispering came to him, candles flickered palely on the altar. To the left a dim chapel appeared like a grotto. Entering it, he felt the chill motionless air. The flames of half a dozen candles burned like white jewels and lighted the smooth cheekbones of a dark saint of his own blood. He knelt before the statue and began to pray.

With the long morning still before him, Mendoza returned home. Suddenly he felt tired and went to bed. His eyes were barely closed when he heard a familiar sound that brought a smile to his face. His granddaughter had come in from next door. Her small bare feet padded through the house and into the patio, where she greeted and nuzzled his son's pet lamb, which was tethered to a stake.

Back into the house she came, straight to Mendoza's bed to demand her morning kiss, then went off and he fell asleep with a smile on his face. Soon she returned, chewing fritto and bearing a cup of steaming coffee. She shared it with him and carried away the empty cup. Again he fell asleep and awakened to the voice of his daughter calling him to the kitchen table for breakfast—tortillas, with hot sauce and coffee. When his daughter returned to her own house, he lit a cigaret and stepped into the patio. A rare cold spell a month back had killed off the tops of the avocado and orange trees. Thought of the disaster made him frown, but tender new leaves were already appearing on the lower limbs in the heat of the morning. He smiled to himself and saw in this revival the fruits of his own loins, daughter, son and granddaughter. You die, but they live on for you, he thought in joy and sadness.

A moment later his son, Julio, stepped onto the patio. His skin was a dark bronze like his father's; his black hair glistened.

"You ate?" said Mendoza.

The boy nodded.

"Good." Mendoza went to a raffish shed in back of the patio where the lamb was tethered and lifted a wooden yoke to his shoulders. Two huge jars attached to it balanced each other. The boy brought him his sombrero.

"Let's go," he said and off they went, the man with his heavy burden, the bare-footed boy holding a cup before him.

The sun was well up now, the streets hot. Mendoza felt the yoke and the weight of the jars. Sweat dripped like water from his face, salt stung his eyes. He had no complaint. It was good to be alive, to hear his son's sharp cry— "Ay, pulque! Ay, pulque!" But now it was a lament, piercing the streets, the sun and his heart—an innocent and terrible announcement of the imminence of disaster.

They rounded the plaza and moved on to the fly-ridden market with its stench, crossed a bridge to a devastated area of shacks and crumbling adobes where goats wandered in the rutted streets. At eleven they recrossed the bridge, sat on their haunches at a market stall, ate tortillas and a thin corn soup, then moved off to the Cantina of the Matadors.

Here Mendoza put down the ever-growing weight of the jars and stepped through the front door beneath a sign that proclaimed this to be the "Entrance of the Bulls." Estaban awaited him within. Over a bottle of beer the money was passed. Mendoza left through a side door, where another sign stated the legend—"Where Dead Bulls Go." Round the corner his son awaited him. Handing him the money, which was wrapped carelessly in a soiled piece of brown paper, he said, "Whatever happens, don't lose this. Put it inside your blouse."

"What is it?" asked Julio.

"Never mind. It is for you, your sister and the little one."

The boy put the money inside his blouse, and Mendoza placed the yoke on his shoulders. I may die, but they will have money, he thought, and nodded to his son.

"Ay, pulque! Ay, pulque!" cried the boy as they moved off.

It was very hot now, the streets almost deserted. At one minute of noon Mendoza and his son rounded the corner of the block where the Mayor's residence stood. Three cars were parked directly in front of the house, an ornate affair of white stucco, red tile and ornamental iron. Nine of the gunmen, including Pancho Negron, stood on the sidewalk. Three sat at the wheels of the cars. No one else was about.

"Ay, pulque!" Julio cried out, and suddenly Mendoza felt the yoke on his neck, the weight of the jars. One for pulque, and one for death, he thought, and the boy called out again.

A short man with broad shoulders and a pockmarked face, Pancho Negron's alert eyes riveted on Mendoza and his son. The others stood at ease, for the pulque-vendor and boy posed no threat.

"Listen to me," Mendoza whispered to Julio. "When I tell you to run, make certain to run as fast as you can."

The boy was puzzled, but asked no question. Again he cried out, and Mendoza glanced at the Mayor's house. No sign of the General. He slowed his steps, finally stopped before Negron and put down his burden.

"A drink, Señor?" he said, taking the cup from his son.

Negron made a face and shook his head. "From that filthy cup which everyone in the city has put his lips to?" The gunman spat to show his distaste.

Shrugging, Mendoza put a cigaret to his lips and, from

the corner of his eye, saw the Mayor's door swing open, the General step from the house. Immediately the gunmen came alert; one hurried toward him to escort him to the car. Mendoza crushed his empty cigaret pack and said to Julio: "Get me another pack at the corner. Run."

The boy hesitated. A stinging slap across the face sent him off. The gunmen laughed. Bare feet padded on the walk as Julio fled. Mendoza heard them and gritted his teeth, then turned and saw the General ten feet from him, squat and ugly, his round face with its two small eyes set deep under his bulging forehead. The face was a brute's, the small eyes belonged to a reptile.

Casually, Mendoza lit his cigaret and held the match. In the burning sun its flame was barely visible, a pale innocuous flare that fell from his fingers into one of the jars as the General stooped awkwardly to enter his car. A terrible explosion shattered the scene and rocked the area for blocks around.

Deadly silence followed the blast. Then the Cathedral bell began to toll wildly above a medley of confused cries. Mendoza, the pulque-vendor, had fulfilled his trust.

PROLONGED VISIT

Hal Dresner

My wife's mother—Mother Harnisch as she likes me to call her—has been staying with us for several weeks now and, since she's just sent for her steamer trunk, it appears she'll be visiting a while longer. I really don't mind at all. Indeed, I wouldn't have her leave for the world. But I will admit I was not too happy about it at first.

The fact was that Mother Harnisch picked the worst possible time to come. That same afternoon the small novelty company I co-owned lost its biggest order and my partner, Herb Baloff, told me he was thinking about taking his loss and getting out. I had too much invested in the business even to consider that and I worried about Herb's decision during the drive home and arrived feeling angry and maligned.

Doris was in the kitchen but I ignored her and went directly into the den, where I poured myself a healthy double Scotch. Testily, I flipped on the television news to hear about the world's troubles, went to my favorite brooding chair and there was Mother Harnisch, sleeping.

It was the first time I had seen her since the wedding, three years before. As far as I knew, she was very comfortable with Phil, my brother-in-law, and his wife, Barbara, and her sudden appearance in my den surprised me. I stared at her critically. She did not look like the standard illustration for a Mother's Day card. She looked more like a squirrel. Her face was webbed with wrinkles; her nose was flat and rounded; her hair was a grisly bluish-white and curled into a tight, wig-looking permanent. I had not noticed her before because she was so small her head did not show above the back of the chair.

The voice of the TV newscaster woke her and she looked up at me, startled, with dull gray eyes. "Oh! Louis!" Her voice had a few nice cracks in it.

"Hello, Mother Harnisch," I said. She offered her cheek and I brushed past it, smelling her heavy Sweet Violets perfume. "You come all the way over from Phil and Barbara's for the day?" I asked hopefully.

"Heavens, no. Why they live over three hundred miles from here! I was on the bus for *seven* hours." She patted at her shapeless dress. "Doris invited me to visit here a while," she smiled. "Barbara's sick, poor lamb. She was never a healthy girl, you know. I told Phillip that twelve years ago but he wouldn't listen. . . . Anyway, I never did feel very much at home there. I know that's a terrible thing to say about your own son's house, but it's true. Phillip has changed these past years, he really has. And Barbara—well, I'm afraid Barbara will always be a stranger to me. Sometimes I feel that you and Doris are my real children," she smiled warmly.

I smiled wanly back, lifting my glass and then I remembered my manners. "May I get you something to drink?"

"Oh, no. And I certainly hope you're not drinking *alcohol*." She regarded my Scotch intemperately. "Oh, I wish you wouldn't, Louis. Alcohol is the Devil's own brew. It was almost the death of my poor Albert."

"Just one before dinner." I smiled, sipping quickly.

Doris came in. "Hi," she said. "Isn't it nice that Mother is going to visit with us a while? I guess I forgot to mention that I invited her."

"I guess you did," I said.

At dinner, the topic of conversation was Mother Harnisch's health.

"The doctor says there's nothing wrong with me," she confided, "but I can feel what I can feel. It's my liver, I'm sure of it. So I made him recommend a salt-free diet and it's done wonders. Now I can't even stand to see salt on the table."

I was just reaching for the shaker to season my salad but Mother Harnisch snatched it from me and dropped it into her pocket. "No," she said firmly. "Now you just try it without salt for once. It's much better for you."

I tried it without salt and didn't like it.

"You'll get used to it," Mother Harnisch assured me. "And you'll feel all the better for it, too."

I did not feel all the better after dinner. Herb's decision to sell out was preying on me and I wanted to relax over a few drinks and think out some rebuttals. But by the time I helped Doris clear the table and went back into the den, Mother Harnisch had subtly moved my favorite chair in front of the liquor cabinet and she was sitting in it watching *Grandmother Knows Best.*

"Now I know just what you're thinking, Louis," she said slyly. "But you just try to do without it. Nobody ever lived to a ripe old age because they drank every minute, you know."

Nodding grimly, I settled into one of Doris' contortionist sling chairs and took out a cigar.

"Now you just put *that* away right now," Mother Harnisch commanded. "Those are the worst things in the world for you and I just can't stand the smell of them. If there's one burning anywhere in the house, my lungs pick it up and I just cough and cough, so you just put it away."

I put the cigar away and sat uncomfortably brooding for a half hour. Then I crawled out of the sling chair to change channels to my favorite western.

"Oh, don't," squealed Mother Harnisch. *Meet the Stars* is on now and I never miss that. Tonight they're visiting with Gilbert X. Everest. You children wouldn't remember him, of course, but when I was a girl . . ."

Our visit with Gilbert X. Everest was followed by *Amateur Time* and then two of Mother Harnisch's favorite "story-dramas." After that, she was tired and, since she was sleeping in the den, I converted the couch for her and then Doris and I said good-night and went into our bedroom.

I'm not a very dense person and I saw the aged handwriting on the wall.

"All right," I said to Doris. "How long?"

She shrugged, pulling pins from her hair. "I opened the door this afternoon and there she was. She really has no other place to go, Lou. From what she told me, Barbara was very unpleasant to her. That's really the reason she left."

"Barbara shows amazingly good sense at times," I said. "You wouldn't happen to know exactly what she did that sent your mother packing and moving, would you?"

Doris' look was eloquent. "She just wants to be helpful, Lou. And she really likes you. She's told me that a dozen times. She'll calm down after a few days, you'll see."

As is frequently the case, Doris was wrong. The next evening I came home to find one of Mother Harnisch's hand-cooked meals on the table. It looked and tasted like baked moss.

"Eggplant," Mother Harnisch explained. "It's very good for you. I have a recipe book that has a thousand meals you can make without meat or seasoning. That's almost three years of dinner," she smiled. "I'm sure we'll find hundreds that you'll like, Louis."

"Right now, I'd like a cup of coffee," I said.

"Mother was telling me that tea is much better for you than coffee," Doris said. "So I thought we'd try it for a while." She caught my look. "Well, it certainly can't hurt us," she said.

"It's a special kind of dietetic tea," Mother Harnisch informed me. "From India. It may taste very bitter at first but once you get used to it, you'll never want to drink anything else."

That was true enough. I took a swallow of the tea and pushed the cup from me. "Well, I'll help you clear the table," I said to Doris, standing up. "It's almost seven and the Bowmans expect us at seven-thirty, don't they?"

"I cancelled that," Doris said.

"Oh?" I said archly. I had an armful of plates but I signalled Doris with my eyes to follow me into the kitchen. With the door shut behind us, I said, calmly, "Why did you cancel our bridge game?"

"We can't just go off and leave Mother alone."

"We'll have the Bowmans over here then."

"And the four of us will play and Mother will just sit around and feel left out? Really, Lou."

"We'll let her score."

Doris shook her head.

"Well, send her off to a movie then." I reached for my wallet. "Here, I'll even treat her to a bag of salt-free pop-corn."

Doris' head continued to shake. "She doesn't like movies. She says the crowds frighten her."

Later that evening I discovered that Mother Harnisch didn't like candy either.

Dinner the next night was broiled lettuce, cheese and chives. We had our Indian tea in the den while we watched

Austin Weem's Waltz Hour, two night-time soap operas and a special show dealing with the problems of the aged that Mother Harnisch knew we wouldn't want to miss.

"This has got to stop," I told Doris when we were in bed. "Especially the dinners. You've got to keep her out of the kitchen."

"She has nothing to do all day except cook and watch television. What do you expect me to do with her?"

"Why don't you introduce her to some of the other old people in the neighborhood. They could form a temperance league."

"I took her over to meet Mrs. Fabell and Mrs. Zworkin this afternoon but I don't think they cared for Mother."

"I can't understand that."

"Don't be mean, Lou."

If everything else had gone well, I might not have had to be mean. After the first week I managed to compensate for my deprivations at home. I smoked twice as much at the office, kept a bag of candy in my pockets at all times, told Doris I was working late so I could eat a decent dinner out and returned home with a full glow on, after watching my westerns at a bar. But business continued to be bad, Herb became more definite about wanting to sell and, in an effort to change his mind, I invited him over for dinner and a friendly conference.

Naturally, I had prepared Doris beforehand and we had a real meal preceded by real drinks and followed by genuine coffee. Mother Harnisch sat glumly at the end of the table, looking like a small bundle of laundry, scowling.

"What if we let Pauling go and I take over all the selling myself?" I proposed to Herb over brandy. "Would that make you any more inclined to stay?"

"Be a lot more work for you," he said.

It was the first interest he had shown and I jumped in to press. "I wouldn't mind. It would——"

"It's very cruel to fire anyone," Mother Harnisch said suddenly. "You said it wasn't his fault that business was bad. If you fire a man for something he hasn't done, it's just cruelty."

"Well, we don't like to be cruel," I said, trying to laugh it off, "but business comes first. I'm sure this man understands that." I turned to Herb. "The extra work wouldn't bother me at all. I could—"

"My Albert was only fifty-seven when they fired him," Mother Harnisch put in. "He worked for the company for thirty-two years and they fired him for no reason at all. They just told him he was too old."

"Well, I'm sure this man will be able to find another job," I said. "He's only forty and very capable. . . . Listen, Herb. We could divide the territory at Moresfield and I could cover—"

"It's a terrible thing to be old," Mother Harnisch said to Herb. "I only hope you never find out what it's like. You just sit around with nothing to do, waiting to die."

"Yes, ma'am," Herb said. I could see he was growing impatient.

"Let's go into the den," I said.

"Albert was a good worker," Mother Harnisch said, fastening her hand onto Herb's arm. "The older people are the best workers. They've proved that. I can remember when he got that job. He was so happy. We had only been married a few years and—"

"Well, if you'll excuse me," Herb said, standing up. "It's getting late. It's certainly been a pleasure, Doris, for a bachelor like me."

"Don't go yet, Herb. Listen to this setup."

"We'll talk about it tomorrow," he said. "Good-night, Doris. Thank you again. Good-night, Mrs. Harnisch."

I caught his arm at the door. "Look, Herb, don't let the old lady upset things. I've worked this all out and—"

"We'll talk about it tomorrow, Lou. I really am tired now. Thank Doris again for me, will you?" And he was gone.

"Such a nice man," Mother Harnisch said as I walked back into the dining room.

"He was crazy about you, too," I said.

"I think it's nice to have a business friend over for dinner and—"

"Make him listen to an old woman rattle on about her husband," I finished.

"Lou!" Doris said.

"Why couldn't you keep your mouth shut for once?" I said to Mother Harnisch. "Didn't you have the brains to see you were bothering us?"

"Lou!"

But I was under a week's steam then and there was no stopping me. I lashed into Mother Harnisch, covering the imposition of her visit, the inconsideration of her restrictions, the atrocity of her dinners and her imbecilic taste in television programs. The insults poured from me like lava and her expression changed from disbelief to pain and finally to outrage and she turned, sobbing, and ran from the room.

There were some slight domestic revisions after that. At Doris' insistence, Mother Harnisch got her apology but with it came the Louis G. Westermere Plan for Household Restoration, a ten-point program as carefully detailed as anything Wilson ever composed. Doris was reinstated as chief cook; the India tea went back in its can; salt, pepper and all the minor seasonings reappeared on the table; the liquor cabinet was liberated and replenished; the candy came out of my pockets and cigars burned almost constantly as I watched my westerns or entertained our card-playing friends.

The only area of compromise was my favorite chair. Mother Harnisch could not seem to stay away from it during the day but as soon as she heard me coming in, she scuttled to the far corner of the couch, where she sat sulking. Naturally, there were regular, almost hourly, promises that she was going to leave; but as far as I knew, no definite travel arrangements were consummated and, as Doris reminded me constantly, she really had no other place to go.

As long as she was out of my way, I didn't really care if she stayed a while and everything would have been almost normal if Herb had not remained so adamant. But my arguments had no effect on him and late one Friday evening he called to say he had been offered a good job with another outfit and he was going to accept it the next day.

"Give me one more chance to change your mind," I pleaded. "I brought all the books home with me tonight and I'll go over them again. Come by tomorrow morning before you go over to this other place and we can make a final decision either way."

He agreed reluctantly and I worked most of the night, figuring all possible cuts that might keep the company above water.

The doorbell woke me at ten the next morning; it was

Herb. Doris, I remembered, was out shopping and Mother Harnisch was nowhere in sight so we went into the living room and began to talk.

It was an awkward conversation for Herb and a desperate one for me. We had been partners for five years and close friends for ten years longer and neither of us wanted to hurt the other. Like vaudeville performers, we took turns standing up and walking back and forth before the fireplace trying to make our positions understood.

"It just won't work, Lou," he said finally. "I feel badly about leaving you this way but if you're smart you'll get out, too. It's just something that didn't pan out and the only thing to do is take the loss now before it gets too big."

I tried again to make him understand that even a small loss was too big for me, that I had all of my capital tied up in the business, that bankruptcy would ruin me.

"I'm sorry," he said sincerely. And looking at his watch he added, "It's almost noon. I've got that appointment at one and I don't want to be late for it. Why don't you give me a call next week and we'll arrange to meet with the lawyer?" He started to walk toward the door but I jumped up and stopped him, holding him with both hands.

"Just wait another minute, Herb. Listen, I've got a new idea."

"I'm sorry, Lou. It's just no good." He tried to push my hands free but I held him, desperately.

"Wait a minute! Listen!" I tried to shove him back into his chair, the rug skidded under his feet and he fell backwards, cracking his head on the mantelpiece.

"*Herb!*"

But even as I was kneeling, staring horrified, I knew he was dead.

"*Herb!*" I screamed, pulling at him. "*Herb!* Answer me!" But, of course, he couldn't.

Then a voice said: "You killed him."

It was Mother Harnisch. She was standing in the hallway that separated the living room from the den, her wiggy permanent mussed and her eyes still sticky from the nap she had been taking in my easy chair.

"I saw the whole thing," she said very slowly. "You didn't see me but I was watching. You didn't even know I was there but I saw it. You pushed him and then you hit his head against the fireplace. I'm going to tell that to the police."

"No! You're crazy. It was an accident. He slipped and—"

I stopped because Mother Harnisch was smiling. It was a horrible, crafty little smile of an unwanted old woman who had just managed to get a stranglehold on comfort for the remainder of her years.

"They'll believe me if I tell them," she said, nodding. "They'll believe me."

And I realized that maybe they would and that I would never have the courage to risk it.

Mother Harnisch saw that, too; her smile widened and her gray eyes twinkled like stars. But to me they were like stars going out, my tiny lights of luxury—liquor, cigars, decent food with salt and pepper, bridge, candy, westerns —all winking into oblivion.

After I called the police, Mother Harnisch led me gently to the den to share one of her favorite programs, *Queen for an Afternoon.*